'You're used to getting your way with women, but I'm out of your reach."

"Not at all," Paul murmured, the warmth of his breath touching her lips.

Kendra stepped around him. "I came to New Mexico to retrieve a suspect. That and staying alive are my only priorities."

"Life is short. Enjoying special moments is all we've got," he said. "Don't pass them up."

"I'm not your type, Paul. I want a lot more from a guy than a good time in bed."

"So you're looking for your forever guy?"

She nodded. "As I see it, the real danger is settling for something less." She needed to believe that, but Paul had awakened a new yearning inside her. It remained deep inside her heart—a temptation couched in two simple words. *What if?*

D0974590

Acknowledgment

With special thanks to the following gentlemen who were there when I needed their help. You're all terrific.

Art Lester, Retired Deputy U.S. Marshal

Duffy Spies, Retired Deputy U.S. Marshal

Sergeant Ryan Tafoya, Bernalillo County Sheriffs Department

AIMÉE THURLO

SECRETS OF THE LYNX

HARLEQUIN®

entertain, enrich, inspire™

If you purchased this book without a cover you should be aware that this book is stolen property. It was reported as "unsold and destroyed" to the publisher, and neither the author nor the publisher has received any payment for this "stripped book."

To Amy Bennett because her cupcakes and cake decorating skills always make people smile.

Recycling programs for this product may not exist in your area.

ISBN-13: 978-0-373-69661-1

SECRETS OF THE LYNX

Copyright © 2012 by Aimée and David Thurlo

All rights reserved. Except for use in any review, the reproduction or utilization of this work in whole or in part in any form by any electronic, mechanical or other means, now known or hereafter invented, including xerography, photocopying and recording, or in any information storage or retrieval system, is forbidden without the written permission of the publisher, Harlequin Enterprises Limited, 225 Duncan Mill Road, Don Mills, Ontario M3B 3K9, Canada.

This is a work of fiction. Names, characters, places and incidents are either the product of the author's imagination or are used fictitiously, and any resemblance to actual persons, living or dead, business establishments, events or locales is entirely coincidental.

This edition published by arrangement with Harlequin Books S.A.

For questions and comments about the quality of this book, please contact us at CustomerService@Harlequin.com.

® and TM are trademarks of Harlequin Enterprises Limited or its corporate affiliates. Trademarks indicated with ® are registered in the United States Patent and Trademark Office, the Canadian Trade Marks Office and in other countries.

www.Harlequin.com

Printed in U.S.A.

ABOUT THE AUTHOR

Aimée Thurlo is a nationally known bestselling author. She's a winner of a Career Achievement Award from *RT Book Reviews,* a New Mexico Book Award in contemporary fiction and a Willa Cather Award in the same category. Her novels have been published in twenty countries worldwide.

She also cowrites the bestselling Ella Clah mainstream mystery series praised in the *New York Times* Book Review.

Aimée was born in Havana, Cuba, and lives with her husband of thirty-nine years in Corrales, New Mexico. Her husband, David, was raised on the Navajo Indian Reservation.

Books by Aimée Thurlo

CAST OF CHARACTERS

Paul Grayhorse—A sniper's bullet had killed his partner and ended Paul's career as a U.S. marshal. Now the shooter was back, planning on finishing the job. Paul's only hope of putting his demons to rest was by teaming up with a sexy marshal who'd already made her own share of enemies.

Kendra Armstrong—Just as she was closing in on a fugitive, she'd been pulled off the operation and reassigned. Was this just a ploy to protect one of their own playing both sides in a gun running operation? Unfortunately, the only man she could trust right now was a dangerous distraction who might just get her killed.

Preston Bowman—A dedicated professional, he was a tenacious police detective who lived for the job, but Paul was his foster brother, and family always came first.

Evan Thomas—Thomas was Kendra's supervisory inspector, a career man well respected in law enforcement. He'd lost faith in her abilities and wanted her on desk duty. If she couldn't bring in the fugitive trying to kill a former U.S. marshal, he'd come down from Denver and do the job himself.

Chris Miller—The former military sniper turned hit man had changed his appearance more than once, so he had an edge. He'd been paid to kill only one marshal, but if somebody else got in the way, he'd take them out for nothing.

Yolanda Sharpe—A young woman with a criminal record and an ex-con boyfriend, she'd made the short list after setting an officer up to be killed. Yolanda claimed to be innocent. The only problem was, her alibi was on the run from the cops.

Garrett Hawthorne—He'd escaped the law enforcement net, though his brother was now in prison. With enough money to hire the best wet-work specialist in the country, Garrett stayed in the shadows, waiting for just the right moment to exact his revenge.

Annie Crenshaw—She'd fallen on hard times and now worked the streets. She'd do anything to feed her drug habit, even if it meant selling out one of the few men who still treated her with respect.

Chapter One

Paul Grayhorse stepped back into the shadows as a jagged flash of lightning sliced across the darkened New Mexico sky. He had a bad feeling about tonight, and it had nothing to do with the storm raging around him.

Ignoring the pain coming from deep inside his right shoulder, he remained focused. The bullet wound had healed, but the nagging ache that remained was a reminder that even the briefest lapse in attention could have devastating results. In less than three seconds, a sniper had taken the life of his partner, Deputy U.S. Marshal Judy Whitacre. Her death, and the high caliber bullet that had torn through his own shoulder that day, had changed his life forever.

He shook off the bitter memory as he continued to keep watch. It was a typically cold, rainless New Mexico storm, one of hundreds he'd seen while growing up in the Four Corners. There was the usual blend of wind and stinging dust, but no rain or sleet to ease the parched desert.

Given a choice, most people would have stayed inside on an October night like this one. That's where he should have been, too, sitting in his armchair, beer in hand, watching the football game next to a bowl of corn tortilla chips and hot salsa.

Yet here he was, standing on the lawn beside an old brick office building in downtown Hartley waiting for an arranged meeting with a mysterious, prospective client.

The skies rumbled again and the ground shook, rattling

windows all the way down the block. Tense and ever alert, he kept his gaze on the darkened street. He'd considered staying in his parked truck, but this wasn't a stakeout, and his visibility and mobility would be restricted inside the cab of his pickup.

Tonight was a first. Since leaving the U.S. Marshals Service he'd worked several cases that had involved teaming up with his brothers, but this time he was going solo, and he liked it.

The woman who'd called his agency asking for help had captured his interest right from the get-go. Yolanda—at least that was the name she'd used—had dialed his office late last night. She'd spoken in a harsh whisper, her words coming out in a rush. Certain that her abusive, soon-to-be ex-boyfriend, an officer in the Hartley P.D., would be at his own home tonight watching the game, she'd insisted on meeting in this tiny downtown park after hours. It was near her workplace, she'd said, and on her way home.

All things considered, Yolanda, or whoever she was, had come to the right P.I. He'd never had much patience with bullies, particularly those who preyed on women.

As the minutes stretched by and the temperature continued to drop, he reached into his pocket for his cell phone and dialed his foster brother, Preston.

Like it was with all his foster brothers, Preston and he had come from completely different backgrounds. Yet, once they'd been taken in by *Hosteen* Silver, the traditionalist Navajo medicine man who'd become their foster father, they'd grown as close, or closer, than blood brothers.

Preston Bowman, now a Hartley Police detective, lived for his job. Even though it was getting close to seven, Paul knew his brother would still be clocked in.

Preston picked up on the first ring and barked his name.

"It's me," Paul said.

"What's up?" Preston asked.

"I'm supposed to meet a client—Yolanda—no last name.

She contacted me last night claiming she'd been trying to break up with her boyfriend, a Hartley cop. He's apparently started using her as a punching bag, so she's asked for my protection."

"Hook her up with the chief's office or Internal Affairs. We have ways of dealing with this kind of thing," Preston answered immediately.

"I suggested that, but she doesn't trust the police. She thinks they'll cover for one of their own."

"No way. We try to keep things in-house, sure, but we make sure the situation gets handled. We take a dim view of domestic abuse," he said. "Give her my number and tell her to come see me."

"I'll pass that on when she shows up, but if she says no, I'm taking her case."

"You're waiting for her right now?"

"Yeah. She's late. She said six-thirty."

"You thinking maybe her boyfriend found out she was looking for help?"

"The thought occurred to me, yeah," Paul said.

"She wouldn't give you a last name?"

"Nope. She was whispering when she called, so wherever she was, she was worried about being overheard. All I got was a description so I could spot her," Paul said.

"Go on."

"Blonde, five foot seven, average build. She said she'd be driving a green Ford SUV, wearing a denim jacket and jeans, and carrying a red handbag. She sound familiar?"

"You mean do I know an officer with a girlfriend named Yolanda who fits that bill?"

"Yeah."

"Sorry, doesn't ring a bell. Give me her number and I'll run it through the system."

Paul gave him the number straight from his caller ID, then waited.

"That matches a residential landline for a woman named Yolanda Sharpe. The address is on Hartley's south side— 485 Conejo Road. Hang on a sec. Here's more. Yolanda's got a record—shoplifting, check fraud and a few misdemeanors," Preston said. "She's served six months jail time."

"Interesting background, but she still doesn't deserve to get batted around."

"True, but I think you should back off, at least for now. Look at the facts. She didn't give you her full name or even the first name of her boyfriend. Now she's late. Who knows what might have gone down? What if the boyfriend shows up instead, mad as hell and looking for a fight? With that bum shoulder, if he comes at you, you're going down hard."

"Like hell."

"Look, bro, something's off. You felt that too or you wouldn't have called," Preston said. "Anyone who checks you out on the internet knows you like riding to the rescue. Remember that roughneck you threw out the window after he cornered the waitress at the Blue Corral? Made the cable news."

"That was self-defense." Paul chuckled softly. "And my shoulder didn't hold me back. He flew a good ten feet."

"Okay, so you're not backing off. Give me your location and I'll join you. You might be able to use a little backup."

"Just don't get in my way," Paul growled. "I'm standing behind the pines in the park beside the Murray Building on Main. My truck's across the street."

"I'm in my cruiser now. My ETA's only three minutes or less, so try to stay out of trouble till then."

Paul hung up, his gaze still on the empty street. His brother was right. He had a sixth sense about some things, and right now his instincts were telling him trouble was close at hand.

Muscles tensing up, Paul reached for the lynx fetish he wore around his neck on a leather cord. The slivers of pyrite that comprised its eyes glittered ominously. He'd never been able to figure out why, or how, but whenever danger was near, the eyes of the lynx would take on a light of their own. Tonight, maybe it was the lightning or the cold playing tricks on his senses, but either way, he'd learned not to ignore the warning.

After checking his watch one last time, Paul decided to walk back over to his pickup. He'd just stepped out of cover when a blue truck pulled up to the curb and the driver leaned toward the passenger's side window. As a brilliant flash of lightning lit up the night sky, he saw the pistol in the driver's hand.

Paul dove to the ground just as two loud gunshots ripped through the air.

Paul rolled to his right, and using a tree trunk as cover, he rose to one knee, pistol in hand, but it was too late. The truck was already speeding away. Making a split-second decision, he ran after it, hoping to read the plates.

He hadn't gone fifty yards when he heard the wail of an approaching siren. A heartbeat later Preston rounded the corner and pulled to a screeching stop beside him.

"You hit?" Preston asked, leaning over and shouting out the passenger's side window.

"No." Paul opened the door of his brother's unit and jumped in. "Blue pickup, turned south down Applewood."

"Make and model?"

"Ford 150, I think," Paul said, reaching for the shoulder belt as Preston hit the gas. "Or maybe a Chevy. The tailgate was down and it happened in a flash."

"Let me guess. No Yolanda?"

"I never got a look at the driver. All I saw was the pistol sticking out the passenger's window. If that lightning flash hadn't lit up everything at just the right time, I would have been on the ground right now, a soon-to-be chalk outline."

"You were set up, bro." Preston turned the corner at high speed, yanking Paul to one side. "The shooter can't be far. Keep an eye out for taillights on the side streets."

Paul kept a close watch on the area as his foster brother raced down the street. Traffic here was light. Hartley was barely a city. Most downtown businesses were closed before six, and the area restaurants and bars were all farther east or west.

"In your gut you knew all along that this wasn't just another domestic abuse situation. I'm right, aren't I?" Preston said as he took another left, then slowed down and directed his spotlight into the darkened alley they passed.

"I didn't *know*, but I had a feeling something wasn't right," Paul said. "I'd just decided to call it a night when it went down."

Preston slowed as they passed a bank parking lot, giving them time to study every inch of the well-lit area. "I think we struck out. The pickup's gone."

After another ten minutes, Preston picked up his radio and called off the other patrol cars in the area.

"So, you gonna report this to the marshals service?" he finally asked Paul.

"Yeah. I have to because Miller is still at large." Paul understood his brother's lack of enthusiasm. Local departments hated dealing with the feds. But locating Chris Miller, the man who'd killed his partner and wounded him, was a priority. "It's been ten months since the shooting, so this is probably unrelated, but no matter. I still have to report an incident like this."

Silence stretched out between them.

"What's eating you?" Preston finally asked.

"What happened tonight matches the prediction *Hosteen* Silver left for me," Paul said. A traditionalist medicine man, *Hosteen* Silver had respected his culture by avoiding the use of proper names. Instead, he'd gone by a nickname that fit him perfectly. *Hosteen* meant mister and Silver alluded to the color of his long, shoulder-length hair.

"You're talking about the letters we all got after his death?"

"Yeah."

Preston nodded thoughtfully. "The old man…he knew things. At first I thought it was just tricks, him picking up on subtle clues, like some savvy street hustler. But it was more than that. He had a real gift."

"Yeah, he did, and whatever he foretold was usually right on target," Paul said.

"So what did he say would lay ahead for you?"

Paul recited it from memory. "'When Dark Thunder speaks in the silence, enemies will become friends, and friends, enemies. Lynx will bring more questions, but it's Grit who'll show you the way if you become his friend. Life and death will call, but in the end, you'll choose your own path.'"

"You saw the pistol because of the lightning, that's what you said, right?" Preston said, then seeing him nod, added, "And the business district was pretty quiet."

"Yeah, but this time, our old man's prediction is going to be somewhat off the mark. Face it, the day Grit greets me as a friend will be the day after never." *Hosteen* Silver's horse hated him.

"Yeah. Whenever he hears your name his ears go flat and his eyes bug out."

Silence stretched out again.

"I'll call the marshals service as soon as I get home," Paul said. "A landline will get me a better connection, particularly on a night like this."

"Better not wait or go home either, if it's really Chris Miller. You should stay at a secure location with backup nearby. Let me get hold of Daniel and Gene and have them meet us in Copper Canyon. For us, that's the most secure place on earth."

Paul nodded. All five of his brothers knew that formation like the back of their hands and, there, in a narrow, dead-end canyon, the tactical advantage was theirs.

Paul thought back to the phone call from Yolanda that had led up to this. He had no regrets. He'd been growing restless these past few months, eager to do something more than watch surveillance monitors, the bulk of his business these days.

Now, maybe, fate was finally giving him a chance to get back to the work he loved and pay his debt to the past. Throughout those long months of rehab, he'd kept going by telling himself that someday he'd find Miller, that it was inevitable their paths would cross again.

The possibility that Chris Miller had actually come after him now seemed almost too good to be true.

"Don't expect me to hide out," Paul said, then after a second added, "If it's Miller again, our face-off is long overdue. This is personal. Come morning I'm heading back to town."

U.S. DEPUTY MARSHAL Kendra Armstrong was nearly exhausted after another eighteen hour day. It was two o'clock in the morning, pitch-black outside, and she was alone in a remote corner of New Mexico's badlands. The headlights of her tiny rental car were the only illumination within miles.

She should have been back in Denver, in on the takedown of the fugitive she'd been after for the past six months. With effort, she pushed back her anger.

According to reports, it was possible that Chris Miller, a high-threat outlaw, had finally surfaced here. Her record for tracking down and capturing runaways fugitives was second to none, so she'd been immediately ordered to New Mexico. Still, the sudden reassignment had taken her by surprise. She hated surprises.

As she eased the tiny rental sedan along a dried-up stream bed, the car's tires began to lose traction. Feeling the sedan bogging down, she decided to leave the soft, sandy track.

She'd traveled less than one hundred yards when the undercarriage scraped loudly, the screech so loud it hurt her teeth. The car suddenly stopped, her tires spinning from lack of grip. The wobbly tilt of her vehicle told her she'd high centered on bedrock.

Kendra switched off the ignition and climbed out. The light in the distance teased her—the ranch house where former Deputy U.S. Marshal Paul Grayhorse awaited her arrival, no doubt. She was reaching inside the car for the bottle of water on the seat when she heard something moving in the brush behind her. Kendra instinctively reached for her weapon and turned in a crouch, gun in hand.

Three armed figures were standing several feet away from her, but it was too dark to make out their faces. The tallest of the three quickly blinded her by aiming his flashlight at her face.

"U.S. Marshal. Lower your weapons," she snapped, shifting her aim to the person holding the flashlight. If she went down, she'd take him with her.

"We were expecting you to stick to the road," the man with the flashlight said, instantly lowering the beam and putting away his gun. He stepped forward. "I'm former Marshal Paul Grayhorse. These are my brothers, Detective Preston Bowman and Daniel Hawk."

"Kendra Armstrong, Deputy U.S. Marshal," she said, remembering not to offer to shake hands. Navajos preferred no physical contact with strangers.

Kendra opened her car door, allowing the glow of the dome light to illuminate the area. Even in the muted light she could see the gleam of cold steel in Preston's eyes, the world-savvy gaze of a seasoned cop. Daniel Hawk had an easy smile, but he stood erect with his shoulders rigid, like someone who'd served in the military. Having grown up with a full bird colonel for a dad, she knew the stance well.

Yet it was Paul Grayhorse, the man with the flashlight, who'd captured and held her attention. Now, *there* was a man who seemed to be far more than the sum of his spectacular parts. He stood tall, with strong, broad shoulders, and had an amazingly steady gaze. Through sheer confidence, he commanded the situation.

"I was afraid I'd bog down in the sand, so I decided to veer off the path," she said, holstering her weapon.

Paul gave her a heart-stopping smile. "You're not the first visitor to get hung up on the sandstone out here."

"I'm glad we're all on the same side at least. I would have hated having to take on all three of you," she said, her gaze studying the men.

Paul smiled. "Preston's the smallest and he can't fight his way out of a paper bag. I bet you were planning on taking him on first."

Daniel laughed. Preston scowled but said nothing.

"What strategy would you have used? Attacking the good-looking brothers, or the one with the flashlight?" Daniel pressed, cocking his head toward Paul.

"None of the above," she said with a tiny smile. "I'm going to need all of you to help me get off that rock."

Paul laughed. "We'll get it back on solid ground for you. Just give us a minute."

His reassuring, confident tone was soothing. Without thinking, her gaze drifted over Paul's shoulders. She'd seen him favor his right shoulder slightly when he'd put away his weapon, so she knew it was still causing him some pain. According to what she'd read in his file, that gunshot wound had shredded muscle and forced him to take an early retirement.

"No need for heavy lifting. If we can get a shovel we can scoop up dirt, add some brush, and form a gripping surface beneath the drive tires," she said.

Paul, who'd already moved around to the back of the sedan with his brothers, looked up quickly. "So you've heard about my injury. Don't let it fool you. I can do whatever has to be done."

She heard the dark undertone in his voice and realized she'd struck a nerve. Paul was fighting the consequences of his gunshot wound by not allowing himself to accept limitations. Although she didn't know Paul very well, she liked him already.

She closed the car door, placing them all in the dark again. "I was more concerned about you standing out here in the open when there's a gunman on your tail, Paul," she said.

Paul shook his head. "No one's around."

"And you know that…how? There's no telling what could be out there in the dark," she said.

"Trust me, if anyone was here, we'd know," Paul said.

"An elephant herd could be out there, and we'd never see them," she said.

Paul chuckled. "This was—is—our home. Once you're in tune with the land, you can see beyond the deepest shadows." He handed Preston his flashlight.

She stared at him for a moment, wondering if he truly believed that metaphysical nonsense. No matter how you felt about the land, no one could see into the night, not without special gear anyway.

"You're not convinced," Paul said, not making it a question.

As his brothers crouched by the car, using the flashlight to check out the extent of the problem, Paul gestured back up the dirt track. "Nature itself lets you know if there's trouble. Look down the road. See that coyote crossing from north to south?"

She strained to peer into the long shadows of night and caught a glimpse of something low, moving fast. "Over there?" she asked, pointing.

"Yeah. If there were human beings skulking around, the animal would have known and never crossed the road, putting himself in full view like that. Coyote survives by staying attuned to his surroundings just like the other animals here in Copper Canyon. That's also how we knew someone had come into the canyon long before we heard your vehicle. Everything became still—too still."

"Hey, you two gonna chat all night?" Daniel called out.

Kendra realized that for a few moments she'd totally forgotten about the car and her situation. Paul's low, gravelly voice and his intense gaze had completely sidetracked her.

"Got a plan yet?" Paul called back.

"Yeah, if we lift the rear tires off the rock, it'll roll down onto level ground. Kendra, you'll need to get behind the wheel and put it into neutral," Daniel said.

"Preston, you take the middle, I'll take the left, and Daniel can take the right," Paul said.

"No offense, Paul, but maybe we should trade places so you won't have to stress your shoulder," Kendra said.

"No need," Paul said with a quick half smile. "I can lift more with one hand than my brothers can with two."

Preston laughed as Daniel answered, "Next time I need to unload a van full of tactical gear I'll give you a call, bro."

"Once the car's free, I'll drive all you guys back to the house," Kendra said, then got behind the wheel and placed the sedan in neutral.

A few seconds later, the car rose and began to roll forward. It rocked a little as they set it back down but continued to move forward.

"Okay, guys, jump in," she said. "We need to get to the house as soon as possible. I don't think anyone followed me here, but you can't be too safe."

Paul's brothers entered the two-door sedan from the passenger side, and climbed into the back.

"Expect some bone-jarring bumps along the way," Paul said, taking the seat on her right.

His words repeated themselves in her mind. Something told her this case would play out the same way.

Chapter Two

Kendra drove at a slow and steady pace to avoid losing traction in the sandy ground. Amazingly enough, there were no more mishaps. Although she repeatedly scraped the wheel wells against the brush, a sound like fingernails being raked across a chalkboard, the rest of the drive was uneventful.

Within a minute or two she saw the rectangular stucco frame house nestled against the wall of the canyon. Moonlight shimmered off its metal roof—a touch of civilization in an area that appeared to be largely untouched by man.

"It looks kind of lonely out here," she said quietly.

"You're a city girl, I take it?" Paul asked. Seeing her nod, he continued. "Life moves at a different pace in this canyon, but there's plenty of company. Big cats hunt here, and bears include the canyon in their territory, too, along with coyotes. Then there are all the smaller creatures. Copper Canyon is teeming with life."

"But no humans beside us, right?" she asked.

"There are several Navajo families within a dozen miles of here, but they're all pretty scattered. What makes this place an ideal safe house is that there's only one way to approach it, and the canyon itself transmits sound like a tunnel."

Kendra pulled up beside the house and parked next to a big blue Dodge pickup.

"You two should probably go inside. We'll bring in some

firewood," Daniel said, signaling Preston and gesturing to a cord of wood stacked beneath the roof overhang.

Paul led the way to the front door and invited her in. "Make yourself at home."

As she entered the living room/kitchen combination, she glanced around. The interior had a casual, rustic, Southwest elegance.

To her left along the far wall were kitchen appliances and a wide counter. A half dozen feet away from there stood a dining table and some straight-backed chairs that were hand-crafted from knotty pine.

Farther in, near the center of the large open space, was a sofa covered in heavy, rich brown leather. The pine frame, with its decorative grooves and diamond-shaped patterns, matched the design on the table and chairs.

Beautiful red, black, and indigo Navajo rugs were hung on the walls facing the big stone and iron fireplace. A smaller one woven in red, black and white was draped over the back of the couch.

"I like this place," she said. "It feels...welcoming."

Paul smiled. "Over the years I've heard it described in many ways. Each person sees something different, but the consensus is always the same. Our foster father's home agrees with people and sets them at ease."

"I love the pattern on that Navajo rug draped over the couch," she said.

"That's an antique blanket our foster father was given in payment for a ritual he performed for one of his patients. Almost everything woven prior to 1890 is a blanket. Navajos had little use for floor coverings since keeping warm was their priority. Then trading post owners started encouraging The People to weave rugs instead. Those were thicker and more appealing to the tourist trade." He went over to the couch. "Touch the blanket. It's soft and very warm."

She ran her fingertips over the woven fabric. "It feels wonderful, and so beautiful, too."

As Daniel and Preston came back in with armloads of firewood, talk naturally shifted back to business.

"I've read through your files, Paul," Kendra said. "From the reports I saw, you were on protection duty, fully prepared. Things went south for you and your partner after you reached the DC courthouse's steps."

He nodded. "I'd checked the whereabouts of the judge's known enemies, including the ex-soldier Chris Miller, the Hawthorn cartel's wet-work specialist. Our intel said he was hiding out in Mexico, well out of reach. That turned out to be wrong. Later, video surveillance cameras across the street from the shooting revealed he'd been on the scene."

She nodded slowly. "Our problem's been that Miller's a master at changing his appearance," Kendra said, glancing at Daniel and Preston who were stacking wood. "Following an auto injury that took place just after he left the military, he had substantial facial reconstruction. The only subsequent photo we have of him is a very low-quality one taken from that video. It was actually thanks to a partial fingerprint lifted from a parking meter, combined with facial recognition software, that we were able to confirm his ID at all."

"That faulty intel cost my partner her life," Paul said. "What's worse, Miller's still in the wind."

She could feel the pain vibrating through his words. Though it hadn't been in his file, she'd interviewed other marshals before coming here and been told that Judy and Paul had been very close. Some had speculated that the two had become lovers.

As her gaze drifted over the man before her, she could understand the temptation he might have posed to his late partner. There was something about Paul, an intangible that went beyond those long legs, narrow waist and a chest any woman would be tempted to nestle into.

Yet all things considered, what drew her most was the mercurial quality reflected in his gaze. Those dark eyes could sparkle with intent, determination, or even gentleness, in a flash.

Paul Grayhorse intrigued her, but this wasn't the time for distractions. She looked away immediately, refocusing on her mission.

Having replenished the fire, Preston patted his brother on the back. "Police work is always filled with the unexpected, bro. What we do only comes with one guarantee—a lousy paycheck."

"We all go into this kind of work knowing the risks," Daniel, a security consultant, said, "but at least we don't die by inches, chained to a desk."

Paul crossed the room, stopped at the coffeepot on top of the stove, and poured himself a cup. "That's exactly why I had to expand my business to include actual cases. Sitting in front of surveillance monitors all day was driving me nuts."

"No one's arguing that, but you should have waited until you had full mobility in your arm again." Preston checked the handgun at his waist, then zipped up his jacket and brought out a set of keys from his pocket.

"You leaving?" Paul asked.

"Yeah. I want to find Yolanda Sharpe, then run tonight's events past my informants. I also want to know if any new talent, Chris Miller in particular, has shown up in the area recently."

"That's why I won't be staying here long either," Paul said. "If someone's gunning for me, I won't be hard to find. Next time, I'll be waiting."

"I can't stop you, but that's a bad idea, Paul. You're too close to this," Kendra said. "I'm here to bring Miller in, so we both want the same thing. Give me a chance to work this case first."

"Are you officially taking over the investigation?" Preston asked her.

"Not yet," Kendra said. "Until we figure out who we're dealing with I'll be working closely with your department, but it's still your case."

Daniel grabbed his jacket next, then nodded toward a rifle case barely visible beneath the sofa. "I'm leaving you my AR-15, with three full magazines. It's got a thermal imaging kit you won't believe. Just take care of it. I've got to hit the road, too. I'm conducting a training op at New Horizon Energy, the tribe's secure facility. Lots of VIPs coming in to observe."

Kendra waited for the two men to leave, then spoke. "Now that it's just the two of us, brief me on what went down earlier this evening."

"You must have seen my report," he said, taking a seat at the kitchen table. He removed his pistol and holster, leaving them within reach.

"Of course, but I want to hear it directly from you, Paul, particularly anything you may have remembered since then." She scooted her chair back, then took off her dark blue cardigan. As she did, sparks of static electricity lit the air. Her shoulder-length auburn hair stood out, twirling erratically, some strands tickling her nose. She brushed her hair back with a hand, trying to tame it into place.

As he recounted the events, Kendra jotted down the new details in a small spiral notebook, noting how sharp his instincts were.

Kendra tried hard to focus exclusively on Paul, but one strand of hair kept evading her and tickling her nose. She jutted out her bottom lip and blew hard, trying to force it away.

"Why did you stick around once you realized that something was off?" she asked, wanting to know more about the way he thought things through out in the field.

"I couldn't be sure that she was setting me up, and I didn't want to bail on someone who needed my help."

Kendra watched Paul as he spoke. She couldn't help but notice how calm he was. It was normal for people to shift and move around when they were being questioned, not necessarily a sign that anything was wrong, but Paul remained perfectly still.

The rigid control he held over himself reminded her of her father, the colonel. Never show anyone what you're thinking—that had practically been the colonel's mantra. She and her brother had learned that lesson well.

When he finished his account, Paul waited as she walked to one side of the window and studied the area outside. "You don't have to keep checking," he said as she returned to the table. "We're safe here. If you're unsure, all you have to do is listen."

Kendra did. After half a minute, she heard the cry of a coyote baying at the moon.

"Coyote wouldn't be indulging its instincts to call to the night if intruders were in the canyon," he said.

"I never heard him at all until right now."

"No problem. I did."

She got the message. They were on his turf, and here, Paul held the advantage. "Strategically, Copper Canyon is a great place for you, but not for me. I came to do a job, and the sooner I find what I need, the better it'll be for everyone."

"Do you have a specific plan in mind?" Paul said.

"First, I need to find out if Miller's really here, and if he's the one who came after you today. I could really use your help with that part of it—but only if you can follow my lead and stay on target. I won't allow my work to be compromised by someone planning to cowboy up."

"I can handle it." He unplugged the coffeepot, then leaned back against the counter and faced her.

"Okay, then. After I grab a few hours' sleep we'll drive back to Hartley. I have to find a way to get the cooperation of the local businesses so I can gather up any of the local surveillance camera video within range of the shooting incident. If we have to resort to warrants, that'll cost us time. I'll also have to coordinate my efforts with your brother and the Hartley P.D. so we don't end up tripping over each other."

"You're hoping one of those cameras will reveal Miller was the shooter or, at the very least, in the area?" Seeing her nod, he continued. "I can help you get what you need. My company specializes in electronic surveillance, and some of those businesses are clients of mine. The others, well, chances are they've heard of me and my agency."

The logs in the fireplace were burning down, and feeling cold, she jammed her hands into her slacks. "What concerns me is that your right shoulder is still giving you problems. You sure you're ready to be out in the field?"

His eyes darkened ominously, and she had to force herself to hold her ground.

"Muscle damage restricts my mobility somewhat, that's true, but investigations are mostly legwork." He paused. "If what's really worrying you is that I'll forget I'm not the one carrying the badge, you're wasting your energy. I want answers and a resolution to my partner's murder. I don't care who gets the credit."

"Tell me this. Are you looking for revenge, or justice?"

He paused for several moments before replying. "There was a time when there was nothing I wanted more than revenge, but I've moved past that. What I need now is to see the case closed and whoever killed Judy behind bars."

Though he remained calm, Kendra heard the undercurrent of emotions in his words. He was a man on a mission, and she didn't blame him. Yet the question foremost in her mind remained. Paul was on the hunt for a man who'd killed someone dear to him. Would he be an asset to the investigation or a liability?

"You can accept my help or not, Kendra, that's up to you.

But I'm leaving here early tomorrow and I'm investigating the case."

"You can't go home, Paul, not yet. Think about it. If the gunman is still after you, that's the first place he'll look."

"I don't plan on sitting around. I'll be on the move, digging for answers."

She narrowed her gaze. "So, what you're telling me is that I either accept your help or you'll go solo and probably get in my way."

"I won't give you reason to charge me with obstruction, but unless it's hard evidence, I'll be keeping whatever I learn to myself." He straddled one of the chairs and regarded her patiently. "It's your call. I've got some great sources in town who'll help me if I ask, but they won't give you, an outsider and a stranger, the time of day without a warrant. If you want answers quickly, I'm your best bet."

There was something infinitely masculine about the way he was sitting, his steady gaze on her. Paul was all testosterone wrapped in a nice tight package of muscles, courage and pride.

"You're trying to push me into a corner," she said.

"Nah. If I were, we'd both enjoy it more," he said, giving her the most amazing lopsided grin.

She glared at him, a look she'd learned from her dad, the colonel, but Paul never even flinched. He calmly gazed back, challenging her with his easy smile and iron will.

This was getting her nowhere, and the fact was, he held all the cards right now. "All right, we'll work together, but I'm wearing the badge, so follow my lead."

"You've got yourself a deal," he said, standing.

He'd agreed a little too quickly for her tastes, but she'd take it as a win. "I'm good at what I do, Paul. You'll find that out soon enough. If Miller's here, I'll take him down." Once again she blew the annoying strand away from her face.

He strode up to her, stopping so close she could feel the

warmth of his body. A shiver touched her spine, but refusing to step away, she threw her shoulders back and met his gaze.

Paul smiled, brushing his hand over the side of her face and pushing away the strand of hair. "There you go. I saw you crinkling your nose and trying to blow it away. I thought I'd help."

He towered over her. Awareness, the raw and totally inappropriate kind, made her heart begin to race. "Static electricity. No humidity here in the desert." She stepped around him quickly. She'd glom it down with a half can of hair spray if necessary from now on.

"All right then," she said. "We leave in the morning. You lead the way out so I won't get stuck again."

"Why did you rent a sedan? That wasn't a very practical choice for the Four Corners."

"No kidding. I flew into the Hartley airport planning to rent something with four-wheel drive, but the agency had most of their vehicles on reserve for an event over at the power plant."

He nodded. "Daniel's training exercise. They put on a show for politicians and investors."

She walked around the big room, putting more distance between them and pretending to admire the decor. Paul was a living, breathing temptation. It had been a long time since she'd met a man who could make her pulse start racing just by stepping close to her.

"As long as the sniper is out there, one of us should stay awake and keep watch. We need a schedule," she said.

"We are safe," he repeated with his usual calm. "But, okay, what do you have in mind?"

"How about four-hour rotating shifts?" she said.

"Fine. I'll take the first watch," he said. "I'll need to be a lot more tired before I can doze off anyway."

As he reached down to adjust a log on the fire, she saw him rub his shoulder. "Do you need painkillers?" she asked, wishing she'd considered that possibility earlier. If his senses were occasionally lulled by medicine of any kind…

"My shoulder aches a bit from time to time, but I don't take anything for it. There's no need," he said. "The reason I wouldn't be able to sleep right now is because I'm not tired enough. I've never required the same amount of rest most people do—a plus in my former and current professions."

"If I don't get enough sleep, my brain doesn't work right, and at the moment, I'm exhausted," she said. "It's almost three a.m. now, so let me sleep till seven. Then you can wake me and get some sleep yourself while I get in touch with your brother and see what he or his people have found out. Once you're up we'll drive in to Hartley."

"Preston will have something for you by morning, count on it. When he's working a case, he sleeps even less than I do."

"One more thing," she said. "If you need to go outside for *any* reason, be sure to tell me. I tend to go on the offensive if an unexpected noise wakes me up."

"You're always on alert?"

"Yeah. When I'm running down a fugitive or I'm on a protection detail, a part of my brain is always on duty."

"Good instincts. They'll keep you in one piece."

As he glanced away to turn off a lamp, she unhooked her holster. Leaving her weapon inside, she placed it on the coffee table within grasp.

"Use the blanket," he said, taking the closest chair. "It's comfortable *and* warm."

She pulled it over her. Wrapped in a comfortable cocoon of warmth, Kendra closed her eyes. Without visual cues, she became aware of Paul in a more primal way. She could hear the even sound of his breathing and enjoyed the outdoorsy scent that clung to him.

Though he was quiet, she heard him get up to stoke the fire. The crackling of the logs and the comfort of the blanket worked a magic all their own and soon she drifted off to sleep. Paul smiled, his gaze resting on Kendra. Although he knew no one was out there, he remained seated on the easy chair closest to a window. Taking off the lynx fetish he wore around his neck, he held it in his palm and gazed at it for a moment. Like all of *Hosteen* Silver's gifts, the hand-carved wooden artifact was far more complicated than it appeared to be at a glance.

Lynx was said to be able to peer into the soul of man or beast and see the secrets hidden there. As the owner of the fetish, he knew that gift was his to use, but for many years he'd refused to accept such things were possible.

Slowly, as his mind had opened to new possibilities, he'd discovered that he could always sense when someone was lying to him, or even holding back. In time, he'd stopped searching for logical explanations and grew to accept his new-found ability.

The gift had served him well during his days as a U.S. Marshal and continued to do so now, even though he no longer wore the badge. He leaned back and relaxed, confident that the terrain around the house held no secrets from him or Lynx.

Hearing the rhythmic sound of Kendra's breathing, he focused on the woman. The blanket had slipped to her waist, and her simple wool sweater, though loose, accentuated her full breasts. Like many women in the marshals service, she did her best to underplay her curves, but thankfully, some things were impossible to hide.

Kendra was an irresistible blend of toughness and gentleness. She was clearly a fighter who'd refused to back down, even when staring down three gun barrels. Yet, in this unguarded moment, she was the most feminine of women.

He'd known all types of females and enjoyed their company, but he'd always had one rule. He never stayed with any particular woman for long. Some had accused him of deliberately keeping his heart out of reach, and there was some truth to that. He didn't trust relationships. Promises made in the night didn't last when exposed to the light of day.

He'd only had one relationship that had stood the test of time, the one with his former partner, Judy Whitacre. The reason was plain. Though they'd cared deeply for each other, the job had always come first to both of them. They'd worked together for three years, and although gossip within the ranks had suggested otherwise, they'd never acted on their feelings. They'd both known that crossing that line would have jeopardized their working partnership.

Paul heard the faint rustling of something moving through the brush outside. Although that type of sound usually indicated the presence of an animal, he'd have to check it out. Seeing Kendra was still sound asleep, he slipped noiselessly out the back door.

Chapter Three

Paul moved silently around the outside perimeter of the house, pausing often to listen while searching the trees just beyond.

He'd made his way to the front corner of the house when he saw the source of the sound.

Paul smiled as the lynx took a step forward, almost as if in silent greeting. The last time he'd seen his spiritual brother had been during a particularly low point in his life—his rehabilitation process.

He'd been wandering aimlessly around the canyon during a long, sleepless night, his shoulder a throbbing reminder of the challenges ahead. Anger and pain, his constant companions in those days, had conspired to undermine him at every turn.

Struggling to find the courage to face what still lay ahead for him, he'd stood alone, waging his solitary battle, when he'd heard the low, throaty growl of the cat. Lingering in the shadows, unwilling to come out into the open, was a lynx.

In the animal's caution, one born of fear, he'd seen his own inability to move forward, and realized then that life was all about choices. His days as a U.S. Marshal were over, but he was still very much alive. He could choose to let his injury define him or build a new future for himself.

Facing the best and worst in himself that night had given him the ability to go on. A few months later, he'd opened his own private investigations firm.

Tonight, as he looked down at the cat and saw the kill the

creature had just made, Paul realized that the animal's focus was his meal. The moment was all that mattered to him.

He, too, wanted to live in the present and stop looking to the past. Yet the sound of Judy's startled gasp as the bullet passed through his shoulder and into her body continued to haunt him. Until her killer was caught, he'd never be able to move on.

He clutched the lynx fetish in his hand until the wood bit into his skin.

"Don't move!" Kendra snapped from right behind him.

The animal disappeared in an instant. As it always had been, the cat showed himself to no one except him.

Having recognized Kendra's voice, he turned around. "Relax—"

She reacted automatically, raising her gun.

Instinct kicked in, and he countered without thinking, sweeping her gun hand, twisting her around, and pulling her back against his chest. With her gun hand pinned to her side, he held her steady, his arms locked around her.

"It's me," he repeated, dodging a kick to his instep.

She relaxed instantly. "Paul? I *told* you to tell me if you left the house. I thought you were in another room and that someone was tampering with the vehicles—or worse! What the heck are you doing out here?"

"I came to see an old friend," he said, noting that she wasn't trying to break free.

"Where?" she asked, trying to wriggle out and look around.

Reluctantly, he let her go, noting she had fit just right against him. "Not a person, an animal."

"You feeding the coyotes or something?"

He shook his head. "No, it's more complicated than that."

She searched the area trying to see what he was talking about, but it was too dark. "Come on, let's go back inside. I don't want to stay out here any longer than necessary. This is the best time for a sneak attack."

"Yeah. It'll be dawn soon," he said, letting her take the lead in the walk back around the house. "Why don't you get a little more rest?"

"Can't. I'm wide awake now."

"So, how about a real early breakfast then?" he asked.

"Thanks, but, no. It's too early for me to even think of food," she said, glancing at her watch. It was a little after five. "Unlike my brother, I'm not a big fan of breakfast. But our father, the colonel, used to insist on it. Personally I feel more primed for work if I have a mug of strong coffee and something sweet, like a doughnut."

He laughed. "Not much for health food, are you?"

"Hey, I grab a sandwich at lunch. My anchor is a good dinner, when I'm not on the run."

When they stepped back into the house, Paul walked over to his chair and picked up his jacket. "Since we're both up, why don't we get an early start and head back?"

"If we start too early, we'll have to wake people up. We want them relaxed, not cranky, when we ask for their cooperation," she said. "Besides, you need to get some rest, too. I need you alert."

"I grabbed some shut-eye before you arrived here. I'm not tired, and right now there are some things I need to do, like contact Nick and tell him I won't be at home. I need him to steer clear of my apartment."

"Nick?"

"He's the son of the man who owns my rental unit, which is over his coffee shop. Nick also cleans for me and makes sure my fridge is stocked."

"With my crazy work hours, the food at my place is usually leftover takeout with a coating of green fuzz."

"So you're not exactly a domestic goddess, I take it?"

She laughed. "Not even close. You know what it's like, working double shifts, pulling all-nighters, traveling the red-eye with a prisoner at your side. When I first started out, I put in long hours, but there was time off the clock, too. Then somewhere along the way, the balance shifted."

He nodded, setting his jacket down again. "It happens like that."

"One day I discovered that whether I was on the clock or not, my mind was always on the job."

"Law enforcement is like that. It starts out as a job you love, but pretty soon it's your life," he said.

"It gets under your skin," she said, nodding. "What I love most about it is that every day brings its own challenge."

"I miss the constant change of pace," he said. "When I started my agency, my shoulder was still holding me back. All I could really do was set up security, conduct interviews, and manage surveillance monitors for my clients. I spent most of my time pushing paper or watching screens."

"And it drove you crazy?"

"Oh, yeah," he said. "I'm a lot happier in the field."

"I asked you about painkillers before. How much trouble does your shoulder give you these days?"

"It aches from time to time, but it's nothing I can't handle. It's healed up nice." Rather than have her wonder, he stepped over by the fire and shrugged out of his wool shirt. "Take a look."

She drew closer to him, started to touch his shoulder, but then changed her mind and dropped her hand to her side. "Through and through, though it must have taken out a lot of muscle. A rifle bullet can do a lot of damage. Rehab must have been tough," she said softly.

He nodded. "It was, but the daily grind of exercises helped me get everything working again."

He saw her gaze drop from his shoulder and run slowly down his chest. Women generally liked what they saw, and he was man enough to know when they did. As Kendra licked her lips, a flash of heat shot through him. His shoulder had taken a hit, but the rest of him worked just fine.

"It's cold. You better put your shirt back on," she said, her voice husky.

Following an instinct as old as time, he curled his fingers beneath the curtain of her auburn hair and pulled her closer to him. His kiss was gentle, coaxing, not forcing, and as her lips parted, he deepened the kiss, tasting the velvety smoothness inside.

Kendra moaned softly, then pulled away, sucking in her breath. "Whoa!"

"My fault," he said.

She shook her head. "If I wasn't working a case I wouldn't have pulled back. That felt…really nice," she said, then took a steadying breath. "Paul, you're a player. I've already picked up on that. But I'm here to take down a high-threat fugitive. Getting sidetracked could cost us our lives, so this stops now. What happened is just the result of tension and fatigue. You know that, right?"

He said nothing, but in his gut, he knew differently. The attraction between them was real, and it was strong. He watched her for a moment longer. It was exciting to see the play of light and shadow in her hazel eyes. Kendra wanted more, just as he did, but she was right, the timing was all wrong.

"I'm going to get myself something to eat. Fresh coffee for you?" he growled, walking toward the back counter.

"Please."

"No doughnuts in the house, so how about leftover fry bread and honey?"

"That sounds great," she said.

An hour later, though it was still early, she'd finished her report, stowed away her laptop, and was on the phone with Paul's brother, Detective Preston Bowman, who was en route to the station from his home. "If you turn up any connection between Ms. Sharpe and Chris Miller I want to be there for the interview. Let me know what you get as soon as possible."

When Paul came into the front room moments later, Kendra was putting her cell phone back into her jacket pocket. As her gaze took in his backpack, she stood. "Shall I follow you into town?"

"I have an idea. We've already agreed to work together, so it makes a lot more sense to ride together, too. My four-wheel drive pickup will get us anywhere in the Four Corners that a vehicle can go. Your sedan—not so much. Why not just leave it here?"

"All right," she said after a beat.

They collected her gear and headed to his truck. "While you stow away your stuff I want to make a quick call to the kid who takes care of my place," he said. "I already left a voice mail for Nick, but I want to talk to him and make sure he got the message."

"Sure. Go ahead," Kendra said, placing her luggage behind the front seat.

Paul placed the call from his truck while the engine was warming up, and a few seconds later Nick answered. "Hey, Mr. Grayhorse, you want me to bring breakfast up now?"

"No, Nick, I'm not at home. There's something else I need you to do. If you notice anyone hanging around my place, or if someone comes by asking about me, call my brother, Detective Bowman, ASAP. Then call me," Paul said, and added, "Avoid anyone who looks the least bit suspicious or dangerous. I've made some enemies, and I don't want you involved. Got it?"

"Yes, sir."

Paul ended his call, but before they were halfway down the dirt road to the gate, Kendra's phone rang.

"Armstrong," she clipped, then listened for a moment. "Good job, Preston! Keep an eye on her, but hang back till I get there if possible. If Miller's at the apartment, I want in on the takedown."

Kendra placed her phone back in her jacket pocket. "Your brother's got it together. He's tracked down Yolanda Sharpe. She's home right now and, according to her neighbor, has a new boyfriend visiting. Preston doesn't have the guy's name, but the description he has of the subject doesn't exclude Miller." She paused, then continued, "The way Miller managed to disappear until now makes me think he's changed his appearance again, but what's hard is faking height. Miller's six foot one."

"So you want to meet Preston at Sharpe's place?" Paul asked.

"Yeah. Let's head there," she said, giving him the address.

"When you question them, let me sit in. If either Yolanda or her boyfriend lies to you, I'll know," he said.

"You sound awfully sure of yourself."

"I am," he answered, feeling the weight of the lynx fetish around his neck.

Chapter Four

Although she'd placed her small carry-on in the rear of the cab, she'd kept her laptop with her. While Paul drove, Kendra worked on the updated report she'd have to file tonight.

They'd reached the outskirts of Hartley when Paul finally broke the silence between them. "I know you've been working and that's part of the reason you've been so quiet, but I have the feeling that something else is bothering you. If you tell me what it is, maybe I can help."

"One thing at a time," she said, closing the laptop. "Right now let's concentrate on the operation underway." She checked the GPS on the dash. "Turn right. Yolanda's apartment complex should be just ahead."

"There's Preston," he said seconds later, and gestured to an unmarked police car parked behind a cable company van.

"From that location, the complex's vehicle entrance and exit are both covered," Kendra said with an approving nod. "They can be blocked off in a few seconds."

"You can bet he's got backup already in place too," Paul said, and parked.

Preston glanced at them as they approached on foot, then got out of the cruiser. "Yolanda's apparently been traveling and got in early this morning. According to the DMV that's her SUV over there—the green Ford with mud on the fenders. Not a blue pickup, obviously."

"Which one's her apartment?" Kendra asked.

"Two-oh-four, second floor, toward the middle," Preston said.

"Have you found any connection between her and Miller?" Kendra asked.

"Not so far. I also haven't been able to confirm the presence of a second person inside the apartment. My men are watching her, and she's been unloading the vehicle by herself."

"All right. Let's go upstairs and pay her a visit," Kendra said.

She led the way, walking briskly. As the three of them approached apartment 204, Kendra pushed back her jacket so that both her service weapon and badge were clearly visible.

Paul remained beside Kendra. Preston, who'd crossed to the other side of the doorway, gave Kendra a nod. She knocked loudly, but before she could identify herself, a female voice from inside called out.

"Hold on, Alex. I'm putting the beer in the fridge."

There was a clanking sound, then steps across the floor. The door opened a second later and a dark-eyed, long-haired blonde in her mid-twenties answered.

Seeing them, her expression changed from a grin to a scowl. "Whadda ya want? I haven't done anything wrong."

"I'm Marshal Armstrong, Ms. Sharpe. This is Detective Bowman of the Hartley Police Department, and I believe you've already spoken to Mr. Grayhorse." Not giving her a chance to reply, she added, "We need to ask you a few questions."

"Show me your ID. Anyone can buy a badge these days," Yolanda snapped at Kendra.

Kendra reached into her pocket and brought up her ID.

Yolanda shrugged. "Yeah, okay. So what's this all about?"

Kendra watched her closely. "You can start by telling us why you wanted to hire Mr. Grayhorse."

"What do you mean, 'hire'? I've never seen or spoken to

that guy before in my life." She took Paul in at a glance and smiled. "Looks like I may have been missing out."

"Are you telling me that you'd never heard of Mr. Gray-horse?" Kendra pressed, watching the woman's expression.

"That's right, but if you want to set us up…" She winked at Paul.

"Where were you yesterday between four p.m. and, say, nine at night?" Kendra continued, undaunted.

"Camping up at Navajo Lake with a friend. We spent the past three days there. The weather was cold and lousy, but it was plenty hot inside the tent, if you get what I mean," she said, giving Paul another smile.

Paul, who'd deliberately hung back, heard footsteps coming up the stairs. As he turned his head to look, a short, barrel-chested man wearing a plaid shirt came into view.

"Hey, Alex," Yolanda said, "tell them where we've been."

Alex looked at Paul first, then as his gaze traveled to Kendra and Preston's badges, he spun around and raced back down the stairs.

"Police officers. Stop!" Preston yelled.

Paul knew instantly that it wasn't Miller. The guy was too short. Though unsure who Alex really was, he raced after him.

Alex had a lead and was as fast as lightning. By the time Paul reached the stairs, the man was stepping onto the parking lot. Paul took the stairs in three steps, but Alex was already climbing into the Jeep.

"Preston, he's heading north!" Paul yelled as he ran to his pickup.

The guy's vehicle was already on the move. The Jeep's tires squealed as Alex swerved, scraped a carport support pole, then sideswiped a parked motorcycle.

Suddenly a police cruiser raced up, blocking his exit.

Alex hit the brakes, sliding to a stop inches from the squad car, and ducked down, reaching for something on the floor-board.

"Gun!" Kendra yelled, approaching in a crouch from the passenger's side of the Jeep, her pistol out.

"Police!" Preston yelled, taking aim over the hood of the cruiser. "Put your hands up where we can see them."

Alex's arms shot up into the air. As he rose to a sitting position again, Kendra rushed up, pistol aimed at his chest.

"Who *is* this idiot?" Preston said as he came around the front of his unit.

"Not Miller, that's for sure, but from the way he took off, I'm guessing he's got a record." Paul glanced at Kendra. "Where's Yolanda?"

Kendra cocked her head back toward the staircase. "Unless she's got a lock pick, she's still handcuffed to the railing."

After Alex had been read his rights, Kendra examined the ID Preston had fished out of the man's pockets.

"Alex Jeffreys, make it easy on yourself and explain why you ran," Kendra asked.

"I want a lawyer," came the clipped, clearly practiced reply.

As Preston turned Alex over to a uniformed cop on the scene, Kendra holstered her weapon. "He's all yours, detective. That isn't the fugitive I'm after."

"Let's see who we're dealing with." Preston went back to his cruiser and ran Alex's name through his computer. "Jeffreys has an outstanding warrant for check fraud and ID theft. He's never been with the department," he added, obviously remembering Yolanda's story about her boyfriend being a cop.

"We still need to know how Yolanda's connected to what happened to Paul last night," Kendra said.

"I'll place her under arrest, then meet you at the station," Preston said.

Paul remained silent long after they were back on the road. "Alex is going to be a hard nut to crack," he said at last. "And I'm thinking that Yolanda may not be the same person who called. Her voice sounds different, for one."

"Maybe she was disguising her voice on the phone," Kendra said. "Either way, it's still possible Alex used his girl-friend to set you up."

"Maybe," he said. "If you let me sit in during questioning, I'll be able to tell you for sure."

Kendra remembered one report she'd read. Paul's first part-ner, the one before Judy Whitacre, had claimed that he had an almost uncanny ability to separate lies from the truth. "Your foster father was a medicine man, and I know there's a lot of psychology involved in healing rituals. Did he teach you how to read people?"

"No, it's not like that." He paused for a moment before continuing. "What *Hosteen* Silver did was open my mind so I could use the gift he'd given me."

She gave him a curious look. "I don't understand. When you say 'gift,' are you talking something supernatural?"

He shrugged. "I can get you results. Do you want my help or not?"

She hesitated, then nodded. "Okay, but I'll take lead. Agreed?"

"Sure." He pulled into the parking lot beside the police substation. "You don't really trust me, do you?"

She weighed her answer carefully. "Intuition tells me that there's more to you than meets the eye, and intangibles make me uneasy."

"Just remember we're on the same side."

"I know. That's the only reason I've allowed you to get ac-tively involved."

"No, there's another reason—one you're keeping to your-self."

His insight was right on target and took her by surprise. She suspected that Paul held the key to taking down Miller. If Miller was really in the area, and he'd come after Paul ten months after his initial attempt to kill the judge, there had to be a reason. Providing she could figure out what that was, she might be able to use it to draw Miller out of the shadows.

She looked at Paul with new respect. No one had ever been able to read her like that, yet Paul had somehow guessed that she'd been holding out on him.

"See? That's part of what I do," he said.

"How? Will you ever tell me how you developed your… skills? I'd be interested."

"Maybe someday," he said quietly. "For now, let's go see what we can learn from Yolanda and her boyfriend. Hopefully, they'll actually know something of value."

THE ROOM USED to question suspects was purposely kept just a little too warm. The subject was meant to be uncomfortable. The straight-backed wooden chair and simple wooden table were other ways of cutting creature comforts.

Paul and Kendra were in an adjacent room with Preston. Standing next to the two-way glass, they watched Alex, who was sitting alone in the room.

"He's an old hand at this," Preston said. "He's only said one word—'lawyer.' You'll have more leverage with Yolanda. She wants to cooperate. It's clear to her that she could go to jail if convicted of harboring a fugitive."

"It's good that you have her thinking about that. I'll interview her now," Kendra said.

"You going in, too?" Preston asked his brother.

"Yeah."

"Down the hall, second door on the left," Preston said, indicating the direction with a nod.

They walked into the room several seconds later and found Yolanda pacing like a caged lion.

"Sit down!" Kendra snapped.

Yolanda obeyed instantly. "You've got to believe me. I had no idea there was a warrant out on Alex. If I'd known, I wouldn't have gone within a mile of him."

"The fact remains, you *were* harboring a fugitive. We could send you right back to jail."

"No, listen, I didn't know!"

Kendra sat across the table from Yolanda while Paul leaned against the wall, watching them.

"You called Paul Grayhorse yesterday afternoon and asked for his help. You claimed to be afraid of your boyfriend, a police officer, but Alex isn't a cop. So what's the deal, Yolanda? What were you trying to pull?" Kendra demanded.

"I didn't call *anyone* yesterday. My cell phone didn't even work up by Navajo Lake," Yolanda said.

"You weren't at Navajo Lake. You were home. You telephoned me from your house phone," Paul said. "I recorded the call, which came at 4:27 p.m."

"I never made that call! I wasn't here," she said, her voice rising. "And I don't have a boyfriend who's a cop. I hate cops. N-o offense," Yolanda told Kendra quickly, clearly regretting the comment. Looking back at Paul, she added, "Dude, I never even heard of you before today."

"Did anyone actually see over at Navajo Lake?" Kendra asked her.

"No, we were in the tent most of the time. Remember I told you—" She stopped, then added, "Wait a sec. You said I called you yesterday *from my apartment?*"

"Yeah," Paul said.

"Then someone must have broken in," she said. "That's the only thing that makes sense. Maybe it was the landlord. He's kinda creepy."

Kendra said nothing. Sometimes, unnerved by the silence, a suspect would talk and in the process reveal something important.

Prepared to wait, Kendra glanced casually at Paul and saw that, although his face was void of expression, his eyes were alert. He was taking in everything around him.

For a moment she wondered what lay just beyond that steel-edged resolve. Paul kept his emotions well hidden, yet she knew just how close he'd come to being killed twice in the past year. He'd also lost his partner, and she suspected that beneath the surface he was concealing a lot of anger. Paul carried himself well and was the sexiest man she'd ever met, but was he also a dangerous man, now on the edge?

Kendra stared at the floor for a beat, forcing herself to concentrate, then focused back on their suspect.

The interview continued. "I'd like to believe that you had nothing to do with that phone call to Paul Grayhorse, but you're going to have to convince me, Yolanda," Kendra said. "A woman called, so it couldn't have been your landlord. He's male."

Paul came up and stood behind Kendra. "She's not lying," he said, his voice barely above a whisper.

Surprised, Kendra turned and saw the utter calm she'd come to associate with Paul etched clearly on his face. With effort, she tore her gaze from his and looked back at Yolanda.

"You said you had a recording of the call I supposedly made to you?" Yolanda asked Paul.

"Yeah, it's in my voice mail," Paul said.

"Let me hear it."

Paul pulled out his cell phone and played it for her.

"That's not my landlord, and not his wife either. Her voice sounds gravelly. But you can tell it wasn't me!" Yolanda protested.

"She *was* whispering," Kendra said. "For my money, it was you."

Yolanda shook her head. "Play it again, louder this time," she asked Paul. As he did, she smiled. "Now I know who it is. That's Annie, Annie Crenshaw. We used to be friends, but she's got so many problems now I can't stand to be around her. I forgot she still has a key to my place." She took a deep breath and let it out slowly. "Now I know what happened to some of my Navajo jewelry. I thought I'd misplaced it, but Annie probably ripped me off. She's hooked on meth and always needs cash to make a buy."

"Tell us more about this Annie Crenshaw," Kendra pressed.

"She got clean about six months ago, then her boyfriend dumped her and she started doing drugs again. She ended up losing her apartment. Now she's working the streets."

"Where does she hang out?" Paul asked.

"You might try the old brick building where Hensley's Gym used to be. It's supposed to be empty now. Last I heard she was sneaking in at night and crashing in one of the old locker rooms," Yolanda said. "But I doubt she's there right now. Once she's on meth, she finds it hard to stay still. Last time she was using she hung out in the alley between the bus station and the free clinic."

"Do you happen to have a photo of Annie?" Paul asked.

"No, but I'm sure you've got a mug shot somewhere," Yolanda said, looking over at Kendra.

"What about Alex? Does he know Annie? Could they be working together?" Kendra asked.

Yolanda stared at Kendra as if she'd suddenly lost her mind. "No way. They can't stand each other. Last time they were in the same room, they went at each other major league and she threatened to have him killed."

"All right, then. We'll look into this," Kendra said.

"So, can I go?" Yolanda stood, looking toward the door.

Kendra shook her head. "Not yet. Detective Bowman still wants to talk to you about Alex. What happens after that is up to him," Kendra said.

They walked to the door, Kendra knocked, and Preston let them out. He'd been standing in an adjacent room, listening and watching through the one-way glass.

Preston nodded to Kendra, then looked at his brother. "So what's your take on Yolanda? Do you think she's telling the truth?"

"I do, which means we need to track down Annie Crenshaw. My guess is that she was paid to make that call, and we need to know by whom," Paul said.

"That person is probably our shooter, maybe Miller, so finding Annie is our top priority now," Kendra said, glancing at Preston. The man was a hard-assed cop, yet he never questioned Paul's take on Yolanda's credibility. Something told her there was more to Paul's ability than he'd said.

Maybe he'd trained with covert ops somewhere, working closely with their professional con men and other highly skilled consultants. Federal law enforcement agents often had interesting, varied backgrounds.

Kendra looked at Preston, then at Paul. "How about going behind closed doors right now and tossing around a few ideas? Whatever we say stays there."

Preston nodded. "My office."

PAUL FOLLOWED KENDRA into Preston's spartan office, which held only a small desk, file cabinets and two folding chairs. There were no photos on the wall, only documents listing Preston's credentials.

Once they were seated, Kendra began. "What evidence did the crime scene team find at the site where Paul was ambushed?"

"Two slugs from a .45 were found embedded in the bricks of the Murray building."

"I was standing with the building at my back when the shooting started," Paul said.

"The shots were grouped tightly, the sign of an experienced marksman," Preston said.

Kendra leaned forward, resting her forearms on her legs. "My theory is that the gunman who came after Paul is probably someone with a personal grudge, maybe someone linked to his P.I. business. With a rifle, Miller can hit a target at a thousand yards. With a .45, he can make a head shot at one hundred feet. The only reason he failed to kill the judge last November was because two U.S. Marshals got in his way. This can't be his work."

"I get what you're saying," Paul said. "When I got shot at last night I was the only target around and I was less than fifty feet away from the gunman. Miller's weapon of choice is the rifle, but he shouldn't have missed at that distance with a handgun either. I'd just been illuminated by a lightning flash—like I was standing beneath a flare. It was an easy shot for anyone with his level of training."

"Maybe he choked," Preston said.

Kendra shook her head. "Professional hit men don't choke and still group their shots that tight."

"Well, if it wasn't Miller, I have no idea who it could have been. Grayhorse Investigations primarily handles routine video and electronic surveillance," Paul said. "The reason I got involved in this last case was because a police officer was allegedly involved in domestic abuse." He paused, then added, "Anyone who wears a badge should be held to the highest standard."

She heard the barely concealed anger in his voice and realized the case had clearly struck a chord with him. Another idea suddenly popped into her head. What if the shooter had known Paul would react exactly as he had and used that knowledge to set him up as a target?

"Who would know that's how you feel about those who carry a badge?" she asked.

Preston answered her instantly. "Anyone who knows Paul or has worked with him."

"That's not going to narrow things down much for us," Kendra said.

"To track down whoever set me up, we've first got to find Annie," Paul said.

"I'll get you a booking photo of Annie Crenshaw. If you need backup, call," Preston said.

"Do you know the alley that Yolanda spoke about?" Kendra asked Preston.

Preston looked up from the computer screen and nodded.

"Downtown, between Third and Fourth streets. Strictly small-time dealers hang out there, but they watch each other's backs and usually see our people coming. It's hard to set up a sting there."

"I hear you," Kendra said, then glanced at Paul. "Street people are usually unpredictable and half the dealers are high themselves. You want to sit this one out? Someone's likely to pull a weapon once I show a badge."

"A lot of people around here know I'm private, not a cop, and I'll get farther than you can flashing your badge. Let me help out."

"All right, then. Let's go," she said, leading the way out of the building.

"Unless we actually see Annie, let me pick who we approach. We're more likely to avoid trouble that way," Paul said.

Kendra didn't answer. In situations like these, only one rule applied. Whatever could go wrong would—and at the worst possible moment.

THEY WERE BACK in Paul's truck moments later. "Before we head over to the alley, let's stop by Hensley's Gym. It's on the way," Paul said. "I'd like to check out the place where Annie supposedly crashes at night. It might give us some insight into her current situation that'll help when we question her."

"If we go onto private property without probable cause we'll be trespassing, and that'll place us on shaky legal ground. Do you know someone who could give us access?" Kendra asked.

He nodded. "I went to school with Bobby and Mike Hensley, the sons of the late owner. I'm sure I can get a key from one of them."

Several minutes later they arrived at a large sporting goods store on Hartley's west side. The place was bustling with customers.

"Looks like a sporting goods store is more profitable in Hartley than a gym," she said.

"No, that's not it. The gym was *Jim* Hensley's dream. He was really into bodybuilding and training. After their dad passed on, Mike and Bobby followed their own interests and started this business instead."

"Paul, is that you?" a voice called out.

A man in his early thirties came out from behind the counter and shook Paul's hand. "I heard you'd moved back home. I've been wondering how long it would take for you to come by and say hello. Man, it's good to see you again."

"Sorry, Mike. I've been getting things sorted out and haven't had time to touch base," Paul said.

"Yeah, I heard. It sucks having to give up your career like that," he said. "You were the only one in our class who knew what he wanted before college. It took guts, reinventing yourself like this."

"At least I was able to walk away," Paul said.

"True enough." Mike took Kendra in at a glance and smiled.

"This is Marshal Armstrong," Paul said, introducing them. "We came hoping you might be able to help us out."

"Of course. Whatever you need, buddy. Let's go into my office and talk."

Once the door was shut and Paul explained what they wanted, Mike reached into the open safe behind him. He pulled out an envelope and slid it across the desk. "The key's inside. Guess Bobby and I should have boarded up that place."

Just then the door flew open and a boy who looked about three came bouncing in. He leaped into Mike's arms, and squealed with delight as his father lifted him into the air. "This is little Mike, guys."

Kendra smiled. She loved kids, but particularly ones close to that age, full of energy and innocence. The thought filled her with a familiar yearning, one that had become a permanent part of her these days.

For the past few months she'd been looking into the possibility of single parent adoption. She'd never met Mr. Right and wasn't sure he even existed, so she'd checked out other options. As she'd researched the adoption process, she'd discovered a series of holdbacks, some due to her profession, and all valid issues she'd need to resolve before she could take things any further. Unfortunately, she still hadn't come up with any solutions.

Paul shook Mike's hand and thanked him. "You've done really well for yourself, buddy. I'm glad to see it."

"My wife, Cynthia, and little Mike changed my life. I never thought I'd get married, but it was the best thing I ever did."

As they walked back out to the pickup, Kendra noticed how quiet Paul had become. "What's up?"

"I've seen two of my brothers settle down and I know they're happy, but the marriage scene…." He shook his head. "It sure isn't for me."

"How come?"

"I'm a confirmed bachelor," he said, then before she could press him for more of an answer, he added, "What about you? Is there a guy back in Denver?"

"Not in Colorado, not anywhere at the moment, but in case you're wondering, I have no intention of becoming one of those career marshals married to the job. I want…more… for myself."

"Like what?"

She shook her head, signaling him to drop it.

"A woman of mystery…" Paul smiled slowly.

The impact of that very masculine grin spread an enticing warmth all through her, and she avoided looking at him, afraid she'd give herself away.

Paul was big trouble, no doubt about it. He was a man who loved flying solo, yet he was built to perfection and could entice any woman with a pulse. Everything about him, from those wide shoulders to those huge hands, spoke of raw masculine strength. The steadiness of his gaze mirrored courage.

"I imagine you've got no shortage of girlfriends," she said.

"I can usually find a date," he said.

She suspected that was the understatement of the year. A man like Paul probably left a trail of broken hearts in his wake wherever he went.

TEN MINUTES LATER they reached their destination, an old brick building just one block south of Main Street in the business district. Paul drove his pickup down the alley, then parked beside what had been a loading dock. The big steel back door had a massive padlock attached to it. This entrance had clearly not been the one compromised.

"Let me go in first," Paul said, pointing toward the door and interrupting her thoughts. "If we come across squatters, I don't look like a cop, so we're more likely to avoid a confrontation."

"I don't look like a cop either. I'm in plainclothes, just like you."

He shook his head. "You're wearing business district clothes—dressy slacks and a matching jacket to look professional and cover up your handgun. You're also wearing sensible shoes, not heels, so you can fight or chase a perp. I'm wearing jeans, a denim jacket, worn boots and a working man's shirt."

"Okay," she said, glancing down at herself and shrugging. "Remind me to dress country. For now, take the lead."

She smiled as he moved ahead of her. He was long-legged, slim-hipped, and had the best butt she'd seen in a long time. Sometimes being second in line had definite advantages.

Chapter Five

Paul unlocked the door, then slipped inside noiselessly. He heard a faint scuffling and saw a mouse dart behind a discarded cardboard box. Against the wall stood an array of damaged exercise equipment, most missing key parts, like the treadmill without a walking surface.

They went through the two-story building quickly, verifying no one was about. Checking inside a large closet, they found that a weight bench had been placed beneath an access panel in the ceiling. The bench was dusty and revealed the imprints of small shoes—probably a woman's.

Paul climbed up and lifted the access panel. There was a built-in ladder there leading to the roof. "This is how she's been getting into the building. My guess is she's pried open the hatch on the roof, and climbs down." Paul stepped off the bench and brushed away the dust, not wanting to leave his boot prints behind.

"Hopefully we'll find Annie before she realizes that we're on her trail," Kendra said.

"If she comes in after dark, she probably won't notice the absence of dust on the bench," Paul said.

They resumed searching and after a few minutes they found signs of an occupant in the men's locker room.

Paul tried the faucet at one of the three small sinks opposite the shower area. "No water, but it looks like Annie has made herself at home." He gestured to a mirror that had been wiped clean.

"She probably chose the men's room because it's closest to her exit," Kendra said. "What we still don't know for sure is whether it's Annie who's living here or someone else."

Kendra walked around and saw the roll of blankets on top of an anchored wooden bench opposite a row of metal lockers. Farther into the room, two matching weight benches placed side by side served as a table. An empty can of soup, plastic spoon, and a bottle of soda had been placed on top of it.

Paul opened the locker closest to the blankets. "Take a look, Kendra."

Taped to the back of the locker was a small photo of two women in their late teens.

"That's Yolanda," Kendra said, pointing to the tall girl on the left.

Paul nodded. "I'm guessing that's Annie next to her. This must have been taken ten or fifteen years ago."

Kendra edged up next to him and studied the photo. "Memories may be all Annie has to hang on to these days."

"Do you want to wait around and see if she shows up?" he asked.

"I don't think she's coming back anytime soon," Kendra said, picking up a small plastic bag on the top shelf of the locker. It held minute traces of a white, crystalized substance. "She's either out looking for another hit or trying to raise the cash."

"Next stop, that alley over by the bus station?"

"Yeah," she said.

Paul's phone rang as they reached the door. He listened for a second, then spoke. "Whoa! Slow down, Nick. I'm going to put you on speaker, then start again from the beginning. Tell me exactly what happened."

"Okay, Mr. Grayhorse. It's like this. A stranger came into the coffee shop while I was bussing tables. He said you weren't home and asked me if I'd seen you around. He had a badge, but it wasn't from the Hartley P.D. and didn't look like the ones the federal marshals carry. When I asked him who he worked for, he said he was a cop with the Bureau of Indian Affairs," Nick said, and scoffed. "But he was paler than me."

"Nick's blond," Paul mouthed to Kendra.

"You didn't let him think you didn't believe him, did you?" Paul asked Nick.

"No way, I didn't want to piss him off. I just nodded."

"Smart move. Have you called Preston?"

"Not yet. I followed the guy outside to take a look at his license plate, but he drove off before I could get his number. He was driving a dark green pickup, not one of those generic white sedans or SUV's, and he didn't have government plates."

"Maybe my surveillance cameras picked him up. Here's what I want you to do for me, Nick," Paul said, then gave him precise instructions. "You got all that?"

"Yes, sir. I'll see you in ten minutes."

"Be careful, okay?" Paul ended the call and placed the cell phone in his jacket pocket. "Because my apartment is over the coffee shop, I want to avoid it for now. Nick will bring me what I need to access footage from my cameras. With luck, we'll be able to make a positive ID."

"Do your cameras cover the area outside the coffee shop, too?"

"They track most of the parking lot," he said. "There are a few blind spots, but the guy would have to have had some serious training to spot those."

"Let's go meet Nick then. The kind of clients Annie's looking for probably won't show up until the end of the work day, dinner time or later, so Annie probably won't be there yet."

"My thoughts exactly."

KENDRA KEPT HER eyes on the rearview mirror. "Nick sounds like a sharp young man."

He nodded. "He's a good kid. He's had some rough breaks,

but he's managed to weather them all. I have a feeling he'll go far in life."

A long silence settled between them as Paul drove through town toward the northeast part of Hartley.

"The guy who's after you isn't coming across like a pro," Kendra said at last. "A professional hit man gathers intel below the radar."

"And seldom misses—unless that's his intent," Paul said as he passed a slow-moving bus. "I've been giving this some thought, and the fact that the rounds came really close and were tightly grouped tells me that it wasn't meant to be a hit. It was a warning."

"A warning against doing what? You can't testify against Miller even if he did kill your partner. You never got a look at the shooter. Are you involved in another case you haven't told me about?"

"No, nor have I investigated anything that hasn't been solved—except the hit on the judge."

She said nothing for several long moments. "I'm getting a real bad feeling about this."

"Yeah, me, too," he answered. "There's more to this attack than we're seeing, and in our line of work, the unknown is what always gets you."

As Kendra glanced at Paul and their eyes met, she felt a spark of awareness. Almost instantly, she pushed that feeling aside. She was here to do a job, and nothing could be allowed to interfere with her work. The colonel had drilled that into her until it had become a part of everything she was.

"Nick wants to go into the marshals service someday," Paul said, breaking into her thoughts. "He's only sixteen and has a long way to go, but I think he'll make it."

"You really like that kid, don't you?" she said, noting the slight gentling in Paul's voice whenever he spoke of him.

"Yeah, he reminds me of my brothers and me in a lot of ways. Nick was in a truckload of trouble this time last year.

His mom had died six months before and his father had buried himself in work," he said. "That's why Nick started running around with the wrong crowd. Before long, he was in over his head. He wanted out, but the street gang was putting a lot of pressure on him."

"So you helped out. How did you deal with it?" she asked.

"The gang leader's a punk with a bad attitude, but I'm badder." He gave her a quick half smile.

THEY PARKED IN front of Bookworm's Bookstore ten minutes later. The hand-painted sign out front advertised their coffee bar and Wi-Fi connection in big, bold letters.

"Bookstores have really been impacted by the economy. These days they have to diversify just to stay alive," she said.

"All the small businesses in this area have taken a hit, especially the mom-and-pop places, like Bookworm's."

"Yet you started your own agency," she said.

"Yeah, but it wasn't easy staying in the black, particularly at first. I've got my pension and disability, and I had to rely heavily on those to get by."

They'd just stepped inside the shop when they heard someone calling out.

"Hey, Mr. Grayhorse." A teenager she assumed was Nick stood and waved, then hurried over to greet Paul. "I brought your laptop. It's over there," he said, pointing to the corner table.

Paul took one of the three seats around the square table and opened his laptop. "Nick, did you look around your dad's coffee shop before you came over?"

"Yeah, but that guy hasn't come back," he said. "I also warned my dad to watch out for him. If he comes in, Dad'll give you a call."

"Great. Now think back carefully and tell me exactly what this guy looked like," Paul said.

"Like I said, he was just a regular guy. Tall, about your

height, brown hair, brown eyes. I don't think he spent a lot of time outside, because he had light skin. He'd roast in the sun. Oh, yeah, I think he had freckles."

"Did he have any kind of accent?" Kendra asked. Miller had been known to speak with a slight Texas drawl. The light skin also fit. Miller was a natural redhead, though he repeatedly dyed his hair.

Nick, obviously unsure whether to answer her or not, looked back at Paul.

"Excuse my manners," Paul said. "This is U.S. Marshal Armstrong, Nick."

Nick shook her hand, then said, "He spoke just like everyone else—normal, you know, no accent."

"Was his voice higher or lower pitched than Paul's?" Kendra asked. People often knew far more than they realized.

"Um, higher. And he talked faster, too, like he was in a hurry."

"Thanks," Kendra said. Reaching into her jacket pocket, she brought out her notebook, took out a photo of Miller, and showed it to Nick. "Could this have been him?"

Nick studied the photo. "Hard to tell. This guy's wearing a cap and sunglasses and the photo's bad. Looks like it's been Photoshopped, too."

"Yeah, but it's the best we've got," she said, disappointed.

"Were you able to direct the feed from my surveillance cameras?" Paul asked Nick.

"It took a while, but I got it to work," he said. "I tested it out, too, so it's all set. No matter where you log in you'll be able to monitor everything from your laptop."

Paul powered up his computer and entered his password. After a few keystrokes, he had the screen he needed. There was a small compass on the lower right hand side. "With this software I can redirect the cameras with the touchpad and conduct a real time 360-degree sweep of the area. If I catch anyone watching my apartment, I can zoom in on their location, lock on the cameras, and they'll track that person as long as he stays in range." Paul manipulated the touch pad to demonstrate.

"Sweet," Nick replied.

"One more thing, Nick," Paul said. "If you see the guy again, don't approach him yourself, you hear me? We have reason to believe he could be dangerous."

"Okay, no problem, Mr. Grayhorse."

After Nick left the shop, Paul remained at his laptop, sipping coffee while Kendra finished off a cheese Danish.

"I've looked at the prerecorded feed from all the angles. He's either incredibly lucky or he knew where to find the cameras and stayed away from them." Paul took his final swallow of coffee, logged off his laptop, and closed it up. "I've also checked real time surveillance, and things are clear over at my place. There are lots of people in and around the coffee shop underneath my apartment, so I think it's safe for us to make a quick stop by my place."

"Why take the risk? If we're going to have a face-off, I'd rather it go down away from a crowd of civilians."

"You need a place to change clothes, otherwise the people who hang out around that alley will take one look at you and scatter," he said. "They survive by avoiding anyone who might be a cop."

"I can stop at the MallMart and buy myself something less businesslike."

"Then they'll notice that what you're wearing is brand-new," he said, shaking his head. "You need to fit in."

"So what's your plan?"

"Borrow a pair of my jeans. You'll have to roll them up a bit, but they should fit. You can also wear one of my pullover sweaters. It'll be big on you, but you can conceal your badge and gun beneath it easily."

"Okay," Kendra said after considering it for a moment. "But I'm calling your brother and asking for extra patrols in your neighborhood while we're there. If the guy shows up, I want backup close by."

"I can live with that."

As she called Preston, her gaze continually strayed back to Paul. Though she knew it would only complicate matters, the more she got to know Paul the more she liked him. After all he'd been through, she'd expected to find a jaded former marshal, sour on the world. Yet Paul wasn't like that at all. He still cared about people and had shown remarkable loyalty to the marshals service and his former partner.

"What's on your mind, pretty lady?" he said, his voice a gravelly whisper that ignited her senses.

For a moment she felt herself drowning in the dark, steady gaze that held hers. Certain he knew precisely how that look could make even the most sensible of women go a little crazy inside, she forced herself to look back down the street.

"It's not going to happen," she said firmly, pretending to be watching traffic.

"What?"

"You're not going to charm me, or tempt me to forget I'm here on business," she said.

"You're wound too tight," he said, chuckling. "I'm just being myself."

She didn't answer. She liked Paul way too much and he knew it. If she didn't keep her guard up, she'd end up in a world of trouble.

Chapter Six

They arrived at Paul's second-story apartment a short while later. "Living above a coffee shop has definite advantages," she said, noting the wonderful aromas that filled the air as they climbed the flight of stairs. "How did you find such an interesting place?"

"The apartment belongs to Nick's dad, Jerry. He gave it to me free of charge—minus utilities—as a trade-off for my surveillance services. It's worked out for both of us, too. Ever since I put up the cameras, his place hasn't been held up," Paul said. "Of course that's not the only reason he wanted me close by."

"I get it. You're a good influence on Nick," she said, and saw him nod.

"Jerry and Nick aren't close, but the gap between them widened even more when Jerry found out that Nick was in a gang. He had no idea how to help his kid."

"So what made you get involved?"

"Nick was headed in the wrong direction just like I was at one time. If it hadn't been for *Hosteen* Silver, my life would have been a real mess. I figured it was time for me to step up and do the same thing for someone else."

"Pay it forward," she said with a nod.

"Exactly." He entered a set of numbers on an electronic keypad lock, opened the door, and invited her in.

As she looked around Paul's combination living room, office and kitchen, Kendra realized that this wasn't so much a home as a place Paul lived in while he worked.

A large wooden desk held three computers, a multifunction printer and a monitor with a webcam. Two larger monitors with split screens and speakers hung on the wall behind and above the desk. Beside them, on a second rolltop desk stood a larger printer and a nineteen-inch flat screen TV. Across from that was a comfortable-looking leather recliner.

Beneath two small windows on the south side of the kitchen area was a counter that held a microwave oven and a coffeepot. On the adjacent wall stood a small fridge and narrow stove.

"It's small," he said as if he'd read her mind, "but it's easy to keep and serves my purpose. What's your apartment like in Denver?" he asked her.

"It's large, an old office loft, close to the federal building. It took me forever to find it. I needed lots of shelves for my…stuff."

"What kind of stuff?"

"Mostly knickknacks and collectibles I've bought over the years. Life with the colonel took us all around the world. Sometimes we'd move as often as twice a year. With his rank, we didn't have much trouble getting our stuff from post to post, but making each new place feel like home could be tough. Eventually I learned to surround myself with familiar things that had special meaning to me."

"You've referred to him as 'the colonel' before. You didn't call him Dad?"

"He preferred 'colonel.' He told Mom that it helped maintain a sense of discipline in the family."

"So he was strict?"

"Oh, yeah. For my brother and me, our house was like boot camp. You did things his way—no argument. Rules were everything to him. It was even more so after Mom passed away. By then I'd turned seventeen and I was marking off the days until I could leave for college. My brother received an appointment to West Point the year before. The first time he came home for Christmas, he told me being a plebe was easy, compared to home."

"Tough, huh? Do you ever visit the colonel these days?"

She shook her head. "He spends most of his time overseas, and a Christmas phone call is enough." Realizing she'd said too much, she suddenly grew silent. Paul was way too easy to talk to; she'd have to watch that from now on.

"It's been a while since breakfast," he said, stepping across to the fridge. "Hungry?"

"A bit, yeah."

"I have some frozen TV dinners. Take your pick—Mexican or Asian."

"Mexican."

"I'll nuke yours in the microwave while you go change clothes. Help yourself to whatever's in the closet. The shelves on the right hand side have my pullover sweaters."

"And the bedroom is…?"

"End of the hall—on the left."

As she walked to the back of the apartment, she found herself wishing she could have met Paul under different circumstances. Another time, another place, they may have become good friends…or more.

Kendra stepped inside Paul's bedroom and looked around. It was orderly but sparse—good thing, too, because it was tiny. The closet, with its two narrow sliding doors, was nearly empty—as opposed to hers, which was crammed full. She looked at the shelves fitted into the sides and saw the sweaters he'd mentioned.

She selected the top one, a blue wool crewneck, and slipped it over her blouse. It was warm and comfortable.

Kendra then chose a pair of jeans he'd draped over a hanger. Like most men, Paul had slim hips. The pants fit snugly on her, but they weren't uncomfortable. She rolled up the legs, creating cuffs, then looked at herself in the mirror attached to the closet door on the left.

She looked more like Paul's girlfriend than a cop now. For a moment, the very fact that she was wearing his clothes made her feel wonderfully wicked. It was like a warm, naked hug from the big man in the next room.

She smiled wistfully. Maybe someday she'd find a guy like Paul who could spark all her senses with just a glance. With luck, he'd also turn out to be a man who wanted the same things she did—a home and kids.

She shook free of the thought. She'd settle for a dinner date where nobody came packing a gun.

When she walked back to the front room Paul gave her a slow onceover. Although she was sure that it was a well-practiced gesture, it had the intended effect. The thoroughness of that look left her tingling all over.

Needing to focus on something safer, she pointed to the tea brewing in a cup on the counter. "Smells good. What kind of tea is that?"

"It's a special medicinal blend. *Hosteen* Silver taught us to fix it whenever…we needed it."

"That's the real reason you wanted to come here."

He shook his head. "It was part of the reason, but not the only one," he said.

"Are you in pain?" she asked bluntly.

"When the wind and cold pick up, my shoulder aches. *Tsinyaachéch'il* makes it stop."

"Didn't your doctor ever give you something you could take for that?"

"Sure, but painkillers put me in a haze, and I need to stay alert. Aspirin helps, but only in large doses. This tea works better all the way around."

"What is it exactly?"

"The main ingredient is an herb known as Oregon grape. It grows in the high country." As he stretched his arm and reached into the back of the freezer for the TV dinners, she saw him flinch. He did it again as he placed the dinners in the microwave.

"Are you sure you're up to this search for Annie tonight? I could get your brother to assign me an undercover officer."

"In another twenty minutes, give or take, my shoulder will be back to normal. Don't worry, I'm fine."

She looked at the pouch that contained the tea. "Does Oregon grape taste as good as it smells?"

"Not by itself. The scent you're picking up includes some other herbs *Hosteen* Silver taught us to add to the mixture to make the tea more palatable."

"So what else is in there?"

He shook his head. "Knowledge like this isn't shared outside family. It wouldn't be appropriate for me to go into details."

The microwave dinged just then, and she didn't press him.

After a quick dinner, Kendra helped him pick up in the kitchen. "Are you good to go?" she asked, glancing at his shoulder.

He moved his arm in a circle. "See? No problems now."

Paul called Nick as they got ready to leave. "Keep an eye on my place, will you? I can't monitor the cameras where I'm going, so I'd like you to stay alert."

"You've got it, Mr. Grayhorse."

Hearing the howl of the wind outside even before he opened the door, Paul turned to Kendra. "You're going to need a coat. Take my black leather jacket. It's on the back of the bedroom door."

He grabbed another, a well-worn, brown leather jacket from the hall closet.

"We're going to have to watch each other's backs in that alley," Kendra said after they were on their way.

"Just stay cool and don't tense up," Paul said. "Some of

my informants hang out on that street, and I expect they'll come right up to us."

Ten minutes later they parked a block down from the alley, then strolled up the sidewalk. Drive time traffic had picked up since their bookstore trip.

They were on the side of the street that was sheltered from the wind by the tall buildings. Comfortable, Kendra fell into step beside Paul.

"Slouch a little more, and pick up some street attitude. You're walking like a cop," Paul said softly.

"Okay," she said, trying to correct her lapse.

They turned the corner beside the bus terminal and continued down the block. The alley between Third and Fourth streets was just ahead.

A tall redhead in a loose open coat, wearing a short skirt and a skintight top, greeted Paul with a huge smile. "Hey, Paul. How's it going?" she said, standing at an angle to emphasize her assets. "I didn't expect to see you downtown. You looking for some fun?"

"Hey, Brandy, how are you doing? Cold evening to be working."

"Pays the bills," Brandy answered with a shrug. "So you looking for a threesome?" she added, giving Kendra the once-over.

Kendra forced a smile, glad she hadn't choked.

"Thanks, but, no," he said, placing his arm over Kendra's shoulder in a familiar, yet casual gesture. "Actually I'm looking for Annie Crenshaw—slim, blonde and a little shorter than you. I heard she hangs here sometimes."

Brandy made a face. "Oh, Antsy Annie? She's messed up. Don't waste your money. You can do a lot better."

"We just need to talk to her. Give me a call if you see her," Paul said, then reached for his wallet.

Kendra figured he'd give her his card but, instead, Paul handed Brandy a couple of twenties.

"You still got my cell number?" he asked her.

"Burned into my memory," Brandy said, giving him a big smile "555-1967."

A small, buxom brunette in jeans so tight they left nothing to the imagination came up and put her hand on Paul's arm. "Hey, handsome, it's good to see you."

"Hey, Kat," Paul greeted. "How've you been?"

Kendra watched Paul as he spoke to the women. He treated them with respect, looking past their present circumstances and seeing who they were at heart—women trying to survive. That kindness seemed to bring out the best in them.

Soon a tall, slender man wearing a stocking cap and a long leather coat climbed out of a parked Mercedes and came over. "These are my girls, so quit wasting their time with chitchat, Grayhorse. Make a deal or move along. Time is money—my money."

"Don't disrespect me or the ladies, Bobby. Get back in the car."

"Yeah, yeah. Talk big. Now look, man, you're hurting my business here, and my girls are trying to make a living. You got five minutes, then be gone before you scare away any customers, *comprendes?*" Bobby glanced at a passing car with a solitary driver. The man eagerly eyed the women, but when he saw Paul watching him, he accelerated down the street.

"There goes a regular. Am I gonna have to pay you to get lost, dude?"

"I'm looking for Annie Crenshaw. Seen her around this evening?"

"She ain't one of mine—too flat and skinny for my players. I saw her coming out of the Excelsior Drugstore about ten minutes ago, two blocks down on Fourth. If she didn't pick up someone along the way, she's probably at the far end of this alley by now."

Paul gave Bobby a curt nod and smiled at the women. "Take care, ladies."

"Come by anytime," Brandy said.

Paul and Kendra walked side by side down the sidewalk, circling the block instead of going up the alley. Despite their easy strides, Kendra stayed alert for trouble.

As the shadows deepened and darkness took over, the wind intensified. Cold gusts chilled their faces as they walked. Kendra pulled the zipper on the jacket all the way up to her neck. Remembering the scanty clothing Brandy, Kat and the other women had been wearing, she wondered how they could stand the cold. Maybe that was one of the reasons they remained around the corner, near the building.

As soon as they reached the far corner, they saw a slender blonde in a furry jacket, high heels and short skirt walking away from them down the sidewalk, her eyes on passing cars.

"I think that's Annie," Kendra said, "but we need to get close without spooking her. If she thinks we're cops, she'll probably ditch the heels and run for it."

"Why don't you cross the street and I'll hang back? Once you're past her, you'll be in position to cut her off if she decides to make a race out of it. Just don't make eye contact. Keep looking at your watch and pretend you're late for an appointment."

"Good plan. Let's do it."

Kendra crossed the street and then glanced back at him. Some men stood above the rest effortlessly. She hadn't known Paul Grayhorse for long, but something told her she'd never forget him.

Chapter Seven

While Kendra walked down the sidewalk on the opposite side of the street, Paul stood on the corner, pretending to text someone on his cell phone. Out of the corner of his eye, he saw Annie stop beside a lamppost.

She turned in his direction, but he deliberately avoided her gaze, and she shifted her attention back to the street. Hopefully she wouldn't hook up with a customer or a dealer before they moved in.

Their luck held. Once Paul saw Kendra reach the end of the block and cross back to his side of the street, he made his move.

Paul walked toward Annie slowly, pretending to be focused on text messaging and looking up only sporadically to see where he was going.

By the time he got within twenty feet, she was waiting for him, assuming a sexy stance, with her hands on her hips, her chest out, her jacket open.

He put the cell phone back into his pocket and gave her an interested onceover as he approached.

She gave him a weary smile. "Hi, handsome. You finally done texting, huh? How'd you like to party with a real live woman?"

"You read my mind," Paul said, smiling back at her.

Behind Annie, Kendra was closing in from the opposite

direction. All they needed was five more seconds, and Annie would be trapped.

Suddenly someone in a passing car honked the horn. "Naughty, naughty," two or three teenage boys yelled in unison.

Annie turned, armed with an obscene gesture, and saw Kendra. As she looked back at Paul, her eyes grew wide.

"You're cops!" she yelled, spinning around.

Paul reached for her arm, but Annie slipped past him and shot down the alley. He sprinted after her, but the woman kicked off her heels, barely losing a step as she ran faster than a spooked jackrabbit.

He was closing in when she suddenly veered to one side, grabbed the chest-high end of a fire escape ladder and pulled herself up.

By the time Paul reached the ladder, Annie was already at the second story of the old brick apartment building.

Paul looked back. Where was Kendra? Ignoring the sudden pain radiating from his shoulder, he pulled himself up and began to climb.

"Annie, wait," he yelled. "We're not cops. All we want to do is talk."

"Screw you," she yelled from above, not slowing down.

The ladder extended all the way to the roof, but instead of going to the top, Annie stepped onto a small balcony protected by a metal railing. Grabbing a big flower pot, she slammed it, plant and all, into the lock of a glass door.

By the time Paul reached the balcony, Annie was already inside the building. He slipped through the half open door and raced across someone's apartment just as a man in a bathrobe poked his head out from behind a hall door.

"What the hell?" Paul heard the man yell as he rushed past him and out the apartment's front door.

Hearing a bell, Paul turned his head down the dimly lit

hall in time to see an elevator door closing. He raced for the stairs, taking each flight in three steps or less.

He reached the bottom floor in time to see Annie rush out the foyer, nearly knocking down an elderly woman at her mailbox.

The moment Annie left the building and stepped onto the sidewalk, Kendra cut her off. She grabbed Annie, spun her around and pushed her against the outside wall of the building.

"Stop struggling, Annie. I don't want to hurt you and you don't want to be hurt," Kendra snapped.

"All we want to do is talk to you," Paul said calmly, joining them outside. "We can walk over to the bus depot, get some coffee, and talk there, or we can do this at the station. Your choice."

"Not the station, please," she said, and stopped resisting.

Kendra eased the pressure on her wrist. "I'm going to let you go, but if you run, I'll catch up and take you down hard. Your next stop will be a jail cell or the emergency room. I'm giving you a choice, so don't make me regret it."

"I won't run," Annie said.

"Good, now let's get out of the cold," Kendra said.

They walked down to the bus depot and went into the coffee bar. Annie sat down first, then looked at Kendra and Paul. "What do you two want from me?"

"We need some information," Paul said.

"I don't talk for free. Show me some money."

"Not going to happen. I'll give you a ride to the shelter, though," Paul said.

Annie shook her head. "I'll pass. So, what do you need?" she asked as Paul handed her some coffee.

"You made a call from Yolanda Sharpe's apartment the other night—to me. Why?" Paul asked.

"You're the mark. I thought I recognized your voice," she said with a sigh. "It was supposed to be payback for you sleeping with Chuck's girlfriend. He said you were a wannabe hero, and that you'd go nuts wondering what happened to the woman who called you. Chuck was sure it would keep you running around for days, hassling the cops."

Annie stared into the coffee cup, then back up at him. "Chuck was a loon, but I guess he was right about you, because here you are…."

"Back up a bit. Who is this Chuck character?" Paul pressed.

"Don't know…honest. He never told me his last name."

"What did 'Chuck' look like?" Kendra asked.

"Tall, brown hair, brown eyes, light skin, freckles, soft voice," she said. "Fit. Not bad-looking, I guess."

"Sounds like the guy Nick saw around his dad's coffee shop. Do you think you'd recognize Chuck if you saw him again?" Kendra asked.

"Maybe, but he kind of freaked me out, so I didn't look him straight in the face too long."

Kendra brought out the photo of Chris Miller and held it up so Annie could take a look. "Could this be Chuck?"

"Yeah…no…well, maybe. His hair looks wrong, and with the cap and glasses… Sorry, I can't be sure," Annie said.

"You sounded pretty scared when you spoke to me, Annie. Are you really that good an actress?" Paul said, watching her closely.

"I *was* scared. Chuck brought out this wicked knife. He told me that if I didn't make it sound real, he'd mess up my face real bad."

Paul didn't say anything, but his fist curled up. "So how did he find you?"

"I was working the corner by Central and Fourth. He pulled up, waved some bills, so I got inside his car. He said he didn't want sex, but he was looking for someone to help him mess with somebody. Payback, he said. He offered me two hundred if I'd make a phone call for him. After he handed me five twenties, I said yes. I should have known he was a sicko…."

"Why did he have you make the call from Yolanda's apartment?" Paul asked her.

"He didn't. That was my idea," Annie said sheepishly. "I wanted to get her into trouble. Chuck said that we'd need to use a throwaway phone because the guy I was calling was an ex-lawman with friends who'd trace the call for him. When I heard that, I figured using Yolanda's phone was a great way for me to get back at her."

"I thought you and Yolanda were friends," Kendra said.

"Not anymore. She won't have anything to do with me these days. She won't even let me crash on her couch, even though she's got plenty of room," Annie said. "Guess she forgot I still have a key to her apartment."

"So you've gone by there when she wasn't home?" Paul asked.

"A few times, yeah, and I took some of her jewelry to sell," Annie said. "Serves her right for cutting me out of her life just 'cause I'm down on my luck."

"A real friend won't let you go downhill without trying to stop you," Paul said, then gave her his card. "When you finally decide to get help to turn your life around, call me. I can connect you with the right people."

Annie took the card but didn't comment.

"A few more questions, Annie, then you're free to go," Kendra said. "Did Chuck tell you what to say, or did you come up with that?"

"He gave me a script he'd written out and had me rehearse it until he was satisfied."

"What about his car? What make and model was he driving?" Kendra asked.

"It was a dark color, black or blue, that's all I remember. I don't know cars real well, but it was a two-door and it wasn't fancy."

"After he paid you the second hundred, he just let you walk away?" Kendra asked.

"No, it wasn't like that at all. Chuck was crazy, I'm telling you. By the time we were walking back to his car, all I wanted to do was get away from him and that knife. He offered me a ride back downtown, but I told him no, that I'd just take the bus. I even told him to forget about the other hundred he owed me, but he grabbed my arm and was pulling me back to his car when a cop drove by. He eased up a little then and I jerked free. I ran to the bus and rode all the way across town. I kept watch all the way, too, but he didn't follow. I haven't seen him since."

"We need a more detailed description of the guy you met, Annie," Kendra said. "Would you be willing to work with one of our techs and help us come up with a computer image of Chuck?"

"If I do, you'll let me go?"

"I don't think you realize just how much trouble you're in, Annie," Paul said. "We're the best chance you've got of staying alive. If I'm right, and I think I am, Chuck's also involved in the murder of a federal agent. Right now you're a liability to him. Without our help, you're as good as dead."

"I'll hide out and move to another part of town," she said quickly.

"That won't be enough. Think about this, Annie. You're a witness who can identify him, and you walk the streets, wanting to be seen. He's going to find you again, sooner or later. To stay alive you're going to need our help."

"I'll take care of myself. The cops can't help me," she said, a trace of uncertainty woven through her words.

"The weather's going to continue to get colder," Kendra said. "You'll be sleeping in places without heat, going hungry, and constantly looking over your shoulder for a killer. Is that really what you want for yourself?"

Annie shuddered and pulled her jacket around herself. "No," she whispered.

"Accept our help," Paul said. "You'll have a warm, clean

place to sleep and food on a regular basis. Give yourself a chance."

Annie looked at Paul. "Why do you care what happens to me?"

"Everyone deserves a chance," he said reaching for his cell phone and dialing Preston. "That's all I'm offering you, Annie. What you do with it is up to you."

PRESTON PICKED UP Annie a short time later. "No jail, right?" Annie repeated.

Preston nodded. "As we agreed, Ms. Crenshaw. I'll take you to a rehab facility. Later today we'll send over our tech. He'll work with you to create a computer sketch of the suspect."

After Preston said goodbye and he and Annie had driven off, Paul walked back to his truck with Kendra.

"What's on your mind?" Paul said, noting Kendra's silence.

She didn't answer right away.

"Something's bugging you, so you might as well get it out in the open. Otherwise it'll stay in the back of your mind and remain a distraction."

"Okay," she said with a nod. "Here's the thing, Paul. I've noticed that you have a way with women."

"You think so?" He flashed her a quick half grin.

"I'm a Deputy U.S. Marshal, Paul. I'm immune. So focus," she added, working hard not to smile back.

"Okay, go on. What's your point?"

"You're a bachelor with no shortage of women friends, the kind who can lead a guy into all sorts of trouble. I'm thinking that it's time we took a real close look at your past...playmates," she said after a beat. "Maybe one of them hired the shooter, and this has nothing to do with Miller. Or it could be a boyfriend, like Annie said. This Chuck character came across as a jealous lover, at least to her."

"You want to rule out my personal life, that's procedure,

but you're way off base there. Only one thing shares my bed right now—my Glock .40. I keep it under my pillow."

"I'm not passing judgment on you or your lifestyle, Paul. I'm just trying to find answers."

"I know. I would have asked you the same question if our positions had been reversed," he said, meaning it. "But I'm telling you, you're looking in the wrong direction." After a beat, he added, "I'm not convincing you, am I?"

She didn't answer. "Kendra, there's something you need to know about me. It's true that I enjoy the company of women. I'm a healthy, normal male, but you could count on one hand the number of serious relationships I've had."

He noticed her raised eyebrow and tried not to smile.

"You think I'm snowing you, but it's the truth."

"Okay, so tell me this. Who was the last woman you were seriously involved with?"

"She's not part of this, not anymore."

"How can you be so sure?" she pressed.

He looked her straight in the eyes. "Because she's dead. The last woman I really cared about was Judy."

She nodded, finally understanding. "Your former partner."

"Yeah." He remained silent until they climbed back into his truck. "What she and I had was special, maybe even one of a kind."

"I imagine you took some serious flak over that from your supervisory inspector," she said.

He shook his head. "There was nothing for him to object to," he said. "Judy and I were close, yeah, but neither of us ever took it to the next level. We knew our place."

"Because you wanted to remain partners and that would have been a conflict?"

"Yes, exactly, but there was also more to it than that. Neither one of us was the kind who stepped into relationships easily. Judy had an ex-husband and a failed marriage in her history, and me, well, all I'd ever had was my foster family.

She and I were a great team out in the field, but back then we were all about the job. Sure, our feelings for each other ran deep, but neither one of us was in a hurry to open the door to more."

"I know all about priorities and how important timing is in life," she said softly. "This job is never easy on relationships or families."

"True, but I loved the work. The first few months after I left the marshals service, I didn't know what to do with myself. It took me a while to find a new direction."

"And now?"

"I like working for myself and calling my own shots," he said. "My only regret is that I wasn't allowed to officially continue investigating the case that took my partner's life."

"If Chris Miller's here in this community, I'll have my collar, and you'll have your closure. I won't back off till my work's done."

"So let's get busy," he said.

"Before we do anything else I need to find out if the local P.D. has software that'll reconstruct the angle and trajectory of the bullets the gunman fired at you. I've got this nagging feeling that we're missing something important."

"It's a small department, so even if they did, it's likely to be an old version, but not to worry. I know where we can get access to a computer with state-of-the art everything." He switched on the ignition and put the truck in gear.

THEY RODE IN silence until Kendra apparently ran out of patience. "Is this a covert op or are you going to tell me where we're going?"

"My brother Dan's place," he said, laughing. "It's like a fortress there, so the added benefit is that we'll be safe while we work. My gut tells me that Chuck and Miller are the same man, so we have to keep our guard up."

"Everything I've read about Miller tells me that we're chasing a ghost. He constantly changes his appearance, and he's good at playing chameleon."

"That's why he's been a high threat/high priority fugitive for such a long time."

"I've got one advantage no one before me has ever had. You're with me, so if Miller's really after you, I won't have to find him, he'll find us," she said.

"You're still not convinced that Miller was the gunman, are you?"

"There's no way for us to know, not yet, but here's the thing. If it is Miller, the evidence says he's playing with you and we've got to figure out why."

Paul said nothing for several long moments. "You remind me of Judy in some ways. When things didn't line up just right, she'd keep digging until something turned up. I never saw her back off a case."

"I'll take that as a compliment," she said.

"It was meant as one."

She took a deep breath, then let it out in a long sigh. "It's hard, isn't it, when someone you care about is taken from you so abruptly. One minute they're there, the next they're gone."

"It sounds like you lost someone, too," he said.

Kendra nodded and swallowed hard. "My mother died of an aneurism when I was a senior in high school. I left one morning for school, and when I came home in the afternoon, I found her on the kitchen floor, dead," she said. "None of us were ever the same after that. She was the heart of our family."

He heard the sorrow in her voice and instinctively reached out for her hand. It was small and soft, and as he looked directly at her, he felt an unexpected warmth touch the cold emptiness inside him.

He brought Kendra's hand up to his lips and brushed a kiss over her knuckles. In their profession, survival meant being tough. Yet even the strong weren't above feeling pain.

When she drew her hand back at last, he gazed at her for

a second longer. "When I wore the marshal's badge I rarely did anything that wasn't connected to work, one way or another, but I loved it. Is that the way it has been for you?" He had a feeling that there was a side of Kendra he'd yet to see. When he saw the shadow that crossed her eyes, he knew that he'd hit a nerve—one she didn't want exposed.

"I am what I am, a Deputy U.S. Marshal who's very good at her job."

He nodded, noting that she hadn't really answered his question. But he was patient. In the days ahead, he'd learn more about her. Something told him that Kendra was worth the wait.

Chapter Eight

"Are we going to your brother Daniel's office or his home?" Kendra asked as Paul drove down an industrial area at the western end of Hartley.

"Both, actually. His home is at the rear of the building, with a view of the mesas to the south," he said. "His wife has been insisting that they buy a house, but I just don't get it. They've got plenty of room. The place is just inside the city limits and used to be a farm equipment business." He wanted to get to know Kendra, and figured her response to his comment might tell him something more about her.

"Maybe Dan's wife wants a place that's exclusively her home—a place completely separate from her husband's work," she said, then added, "And who wants their kitchen to be a converted tractor showroom?"

Paul shrugged. "It sounds like you agree with my sister-in-law."

"I do. When I put away my gun at night, I want to relax in a setting that reminds me that I'm more than my work. My place is peaceful, filled with things that reflect the other side of me—the woman without the badge."

"When I was with the service, the work *was* my life," Paul said.

"And you still sleep in what's basically your office, so you haven't changed much," she said, flashing him a quick smile.

"But I need the separation. Of course, there are times when work doesn't allow you any down time."

"Tell me about it," he said, laughing.

They arrived at Daniel's complex ten minutes later. Paul stopped, twenty feet from the metal gate that stood at the end of a driveway dividing two dark expanses he knew to be alfalfa fields.

"The lock looks like its impossible to tamper with, embedded in that big concrete post. What do you do, punch in a code?" she asked.

"Yeah, Dan's setup defeats bolt cutters or torches. Take a look."

As Paul looked past the gate toward Daniel's place, he felt the lynx fetish around his neck grow heavier. He pulled it out, thinking it had become caught in his sweater, but when he did, he saw the lynx's eyes glimmer.

He tensed and looked back toward the highway, where there was a lot of ground cover. Out of the corner of his eye he could see that Kendra's attention was focused elsewhere, and she'd wandered over close to the gate.

"It's so dark I can't even see my shoes." She reached for the penlight in her pocket, but her cell phone came out too and fell to the ground. "Crap. Where'd it go?"

He glanced over at her. "Need my help?"

"No, think I found it." As she bent over to pick up her phone, Paul caught a flash of movement in the brush to his left, then a faint beam of red light illuminated by road dust. Turning, he discovered the bright ruby dot of a laser sight on the gate just above Kendra's back.

"Gun!" he yelled, racing toward her. Faint pops came from the field to their left, and they both dove to the ground.

Paul rolled onto his side, grabbed his Glock, then returned fire, aiming low to avoid reaching the highway beyond. Kendra also fired her weapon, twice.

The attack stopped as abruptly as it had begun. They held

fire, then remained motionless, listening and searching the night for a target. About twenty seconds later, they heard a car motor revving up in the distance.

"Cover me!" Paul yelled, jumping to his feet. He ran in a zigzag pattern down the road, searching across the field for the vehicle. When he finally reached the cattle guard, it was too late to get off a shot. All he could see was the red taillights and rear end of a green car—no plate—screeching down the highway.

He cursed, then turned to look at Kendra, who'd run with him and stopped a dozen feet behind him. "You okay?" he asked, stepping closer.

She returned her pistol to the holster at her hip, then reached up to touch her cheek. "Gravel and a scrape, but no gushing blood, so I guess I'm in one piece," she said thinly. As she turned up the collar of her jacket, shielding herself from the wind, she inhaled sharply.

"What's wrong?" he asked instantly.

"I'm not sure…maybe I'm wrong." She slipped off Paul's jacket and held it up in the moonlight for a closer inspection. There was a small hole at the back of the collar. "I wasn't wrong. That buzzing that grazed my face—it *was* a bullet."

Paul placed his hands on her shoulders, looking her over carefully. "Good thing you dropped your phone."

"By yelling at me when you did, you probably saved my life," she said, trying not to shake. "I'm a deputy marshal and I've had people shoot at me before, but no one's ever come this close."

The gate swung open with a loud squeak and they turned to find Daniel rushing forward in a crouch, assault rifle in one hand. "Get inside quickly."

"He's long gone, bro," Paul said, shifting his shoulder and biting back a groan at a spasm of pain.

"Come on," he said. "Hurry up anyway."

Less than two minutes later they were inside the big metal building, standing well away from the windows.

Daniel glanced over at his brother. "What is it with you, bro? You're a real bullet magnet these days."

"Thank you, I'm fine," Paul shot back.

"Hey, am I wrong?"

"This time, I wasn't the target," he said, then glanced at Kendra.

She brushed the gravel from her cell phone with an unsteady hand. "We need to call the Hartley P.D."

"Already done," Daniel said. "I'm also calling in some family help."

Kendra sat on the leather couch and opened her phone, verifying it still worked. "If Paul hadn't pushed me to one side when he did, the sniper would have locked in on me for sure."

"Fate always has the last word," Daniel said.

"This…incident," she said slowly and swallowed hard. "It's given me an idea, and a new angle we can pursue."

Paul knew she was using police speak to help her push back her fear and bring herself back under control. He'd had to do the same thing countless times when he'd worn the badge.

"So fill me in," he said.

"I will, but first I have to report what's happened to my supervisor in Denver."

KENDRA STOOD IN an adjacent office. Alone, she took several deep breaths before making the call. Once she was ready, she dialed and spoke to her supervisory inspector, Evan Thomas.

Kendra paid particular attention to the details, keeping any hint of emotion out of her voice. It was part of her training, and she knew what was expected of her.

"If you're really up against Miller, then I'm guessing he was aiming for Grayhorse, but you got in the way," Thomas said in a flat, no-nonsense tone. "Of course, if Miller found out that a marshal had been sent there to bring him in, it's also possible he targeted *you* first. You're the bigger threat."

"Well, Paul was closer, yet the rounds seemed directed at me, not him. This was the work of a professional, at least in my experience. I think he *was* after me."

"Don't rely on just your gut. You said there was a breeze, and the perp used a silencer. Wind and the low velocity of a suppressed round make for inaccuracy, and it was dark. Work with the Hartley crime scene people, check out the evidence, and see what you can come up with, then we'll talk again."

Kendra hung up, her thoughts racing. She'd been scared before, but now she was angry. She did trust her gut, and whoever had come after her was going down. After that initial burst of fear, only adrenaline remained.

She was pumped and ready for action. As a Deputy U.S. Marshal, she'd put some really dangerous men behind bars and made the world a little safer for everyone else. It was time for her to do what she did best.

Feeling more confident, she took a few moments for herself.

No matter how bad things got, she loved her work. What she did every day made a difference, and that's what kept her going.

Of course someday she'd have to make a choice—her work as a marshal or becoming a single mom. The crazy hours and the danger were all part of what had drawn her to the job, but her child would need security and deserved a parent who'd be home more often than not. That was one of the holdbacks she'd yet to figure out.

Sooner or later she'd have to find a new career, hopefully one that wouldn't make her feel she was just punching a time clock somewhere. She'd never be able to open an electronic security firm like Paul's. The work was too routine. Watching monitors or doing background checks all day would make her crazy. She was made for more active work, and if she didn't remain true to herself, what kind of mom could she hope to be?

She shook her head. All that could wait. Right now she had work to do.

As she stepped back into the hall, Paul was there to meet her. "My brother Preston is here now to help out. What's the news from Denver?"

"Evan Thomas, my supervisory inspector, thinks you were probably the primary target, but I got in the way and needed to be taken out."

Paul said nothing for a moment, his gaze so steady it was unnerving. He seemed to be looking right into her soul.

"Yeah, and I know Thomas and where he's coming from. But you know he's wrong, and you've got solid reasons for believing that."

Paul was right on target. He could read her thoughts with amazing accuracy, and it was a bit unnerving. "You were a Deputy U.S. Marshal once, Paul. You know there are details I can't discuss, not even with you."

"You still need help, Kendra, and you're going to have to start thinking outside the box. My record's spotless. You can trust me. Talk to me."

"Not here."

"Yes, here. My brothers are the most reliable backup you can possibly hope to have, but we can't work with you effectively if you're going to keep information from us." He paused and took a long breath. "I know you've read my brothers' files. They're men of honor. If we're going to stand in the line of fire, we deserve to know what's going on."

It took her several beats, but at length, she nodded. He had a point.

As they entered the room where two of Paul's brothers— Daniel and Preston—were waiting, she'd already decided that trusting them was the only way to go.

Kendra sat down at the big conference table and looked at

the men already seated there, coffee mugs in hand. As Paul suspected, she'd read all their files. She knew about each of Paul's foster brothers.

Besides Preston, the city cop, and Daniel, the business security expert, there was Kyle, who was with the NCIS at Diego Garcia. Rick was with the FBI, but his current overseas work—location not listed—had been redacted in the one paragraph summary she'd been able to access. Reading between the lines, she assumed Rick was working undercover. All of the men, raised in a foster home by a tribal medicine man, were connected to law enforcement in some way. All except for Gene, who was a truck driver turned rancher in southwestern Colorado. From the documents she'd seen, they were a tight-knit group, and she could certainly use trained, trustworthy manpower.

"I'm going to need some help, guys, but what I say here today can't leave this room." She took the offered mug of hot coffee.

Paul looked at her and nodded.

Daniel did the same.

Only Preston hesitated. "I can't withhold information from my P.D., not if it's something that affects them directly."

"I understand, but this has more to do with the marshals service than it does with your department."

"Come on, Preston. I need you in on this," Paul said.

She saw the look that passed between both men and knew that nothing would ever trump their loyalty to each other.

"All right," Preston said at last. "I'm in."

Kendra nodded, and with a steady voice began. "The shooter who came after me tonight may be linked to a case I was working before coming here. He and Miller may even be working together."

It took her a moment to gather her thoughts, but no one interrupted the silence. Grateful, she considered her words carefully. The colonel and the marshals service had taught her to present facts as clearly and as succinctly as possible, leaving emotion—in this case her fears and sense of betrayal—out of the narrative.

"Before I was sent here to search for Chris Miller, I was working a different fugitive retrieval case. The felon I was after, John Lester, is a convicted gunrunner and a suspected member of the Hawthorn cartel. He served six months, then broke out of a Texas lockup. Since then he's always remained a step ahead of us. Last time we got a lead, I prepared for the takedown by restricting information to our office only. I also held off filing any reports that would give away the salient details. There was no way Lester could have guessed our next move, yet somehow he was tipped off. By the time we got to where he'd been staying, the only things left were his fingerprints."

Paul, Daniel and Preston exchanged glances again, but remained silent.

Kendra continued. "That's when I began to suspect we had an informant in our offices, someone inside the service," she said. "In view of what's happened, I think it's possible I was taken off that case because someone wanted me out of the way. Miller is the Hawthorn cartel's wet-work specialist, and Lester is a gunrunner for them. That connection may explain why I'm now a target."

"But what you've said also leads back to me," Paul said. "The judge my partner and I were protecting was presiding over Mark Hawthorn's trial. He's Garrett Hawthorn's brother, the leader of the Hawthorn cartel. I'm in the crosshairs because I prevented the death of the judge, and Mark was eventually convicted of murder."

"Do you have any evidence that proves the Hawthorn cartel has an informant inside the marshals service?" Preston asked.

Kendra shook her head. "All I've got is this. Right before I was sent here, while I was still hot on Lester's trail, I spotted someone tailing me after hours. I tried to double back more than once to catch the guy, but he was good, and I never did get a look at him—or her. I finally fell back on procedure and reported it."

Preston nodded approvingly. "Sometimes following protocol is the only way to go."

She shrugged. "Evan Thomas, my supervisory inspector, put two deputy marshals on me, but they couldn't find any evidence that I was being followed. Neither did I. Eventually I was called to Evan's office. The consensus that came down the chain of command was that I'd been working the Lester case too long and hard. I was given a choice. I could take leave and see the shrink, or accept another case, like the hunt for Miller."

"You were making certain people nervous," Paul said.

"Yeah, that's the way I saw it, too, but all I had was a gut feeling and a few random glances at a careful stalker—a man."

"Could it have been Miller?" Paul asked.

"Maybe, I only got a glimpse or two. Without solid evidence, there was no way for me to prove any of it. But the guy had some serious training. Three of us couldn't work him into a corner."

"And now your supervisory inspector is assuming you're paranoid," Preston said. "But based solely on the facts, his theory about tonight's shooting at least has some merit. In the shooter's eyes, Paul's an easier target once his backup is taken out."

She shook her head. "Experienced snipers learn to focus and filter out distractions. If Paul had been his target, the bullets would have been directed toward him first. He wouldn't have wasted the opportunity to take him out. More details— Paul was closer, and I was moving away from the shooter's location. If Paul was the target, I certainly wasn't in the way, blocking his line of fire. If anything, it was the other way around."

"I agree with your conclusions," Daniel said.

"So here's what I think we should do, though admittedly, it carries some risk," she said. "I want to gather up photos of local criminals with the right weapons training and background, then take those to Annie. Let's see if she can ID any of them as 'Chuck.' If she can't, then we go back to searching for Miller."

"That's a good idea," Paul said.

"Why don't you access the photos from my computer here?" Daniel asked Preston.

"Yeah, might as well. It'll save time," he said.

"I'm going to call the rehab center and get an update on Annie," Paul said, reaching for his cell phone and moving away.

Kendra remained with Preston and Daniel, and a few minutes later, Paul rejoined them, a somber look on his face. "Bad news."

Something in his tone made Kendra's blood turn to ice. "What's wrong?"

"Annie's gone."

Chapter Nine

Kendra swallowed hard. "What do you mean 'gone'?"

"It looks like she just split," Paul said. "She was at a group counseling session when she excused herself. They never saw her after that, so they think she may have slipped out the side door."

"That wouldn't have been hard to do," Preston said. "She was in protective custody—she wasn't a prisoner. A street-wise person like Annie Crenshaw would have found it easy to give them the slip."

"The center reported her absence to the P.D. about an hour ago. The D.A. was notified since Annie is a material witness to a crime," Paul said. "Officers checked out the gym where she'd been crashing, but they didn't find her."

"What about her cell phone?" Kendra asked. "Let me call her, or better yet, Paul, you do it. You had more of a connection with her."

He dialed, but no one answered. "All I'm getting is her voice mail. Let's stop by the alley where we first found her. Maybe she's working the streets again. Or maybe we can find somebody who's seen her and pick up a fresh lead."

"Good idea," Kendra said. "Let's go."

"I'll put a BOLO out on her," Preston said.

Daniel was the last to speak. "Wait a minute, guys. I've got an idea. Give me her cell number, Paul. If her phone's still on, I may be able to track the signal."

"You've got equipment that can do that?" Kendra looked over, eyebrows raised.

Daniel shrugged.

"Don't ask," Paul said, leading Kendra to the door. "Let's go. If he gets something, he'll let us know."

They were on their way a short time later. "We'll be getting there while people are still out on the streets so that'll help. If she's not there, we can ask around," she said.

They arrived a short time later and walked the alley from Third to Fourth Street, but couldn't locate Annie. Although they searched the area themselves and talked to the working girls, no one had seen her.

Soon they began cruising the neighboring streets in Paul's truck. There was heavy traffic around a city park sheltered on all four sides by multiple-story buildings.

"This is a good place for the street people to hang out away from the cold," he said.

"This park is more sheltered than the area around Fourth Street. With those scanty outfits, the women must be freezing this evening," she said. "I just don't understand what makes them choose the life."

"They tell themselves it's temporary, and that things are going to change for them real soon. That hope is sometimes all they've got to hold on to. Remember the movie *Pretty Woman?* The little girl who dares to dream of bigger and better things is still inside these women. That's what gets them through the day."

It was the gentling of his voice that captured her attention most. The way he'd treated Brandy and the others may have been rooted in something more than compassion. She had a strong feeling that there was a lot more to Paul's story. She wanted to ask him about it, but this wasn't the time for distractions.

"There's Kat, the brunette we saw before," Kendra said. "She just came out of that apartment building."

Paul pulled over to the curb. Kat and two other women were standing near the street corner as he and Kendra approached.

Kat looked over at them and managed a shaky smile. "Slow, cold night," she said, crossing her arms in front of her chest. "You still looking for Annie?"

Paul nodded. "Have you seen her?"

"She came by about ten minutes ago. She said she needed quick cash to get out of town. Got lucky, I guess, 'cause she scored a 'date' almost immediately."

"You get a good look at the vehicle—and the john?" Kendra pressed.

"It was an old van, Chevy or a Dodge. The guy had a beard, neatly trimmed, matching dark hair and wire-rimmed glasses."

"What about the van? Can you describe it?" Paul asked her.

"Like from the eighties. It was faded blue with one of those chrome ladders in the back and a luggage rack on the roof."

"Did you happen to catch the license plate?" Paul asked.

"No, sorry," she said, shivering.

Paul fished a few bills from his wallet. "Here you go, Kat. Call it a night, go home, and get warm."

"Thanks, Paul. If you ever need anything, information… or whatever…just drop by."

"Take care of yourself, Kat."

As she walked off, Kendra gave Paul a gentle smile. "You're not an undercover minister or something like that, right?"

He shook his head, chuckling. "No. I just know what it's like to be alone, miserable and afraid. It's something you never forget."

She wanted to know more, above and beyond the cold compilation of facts that were in his file, but before she could ask, he got down to business again.

"We need to work this block and talk to anyone who might have seen that van," he said.

"Let's split up. It'll go faster."

Kendra asked everyone she saw on her side of the street, but no one wanted to talk to her or get involved. By the time she joined Paul again, she knew at a glance he had nothing new to share either.

"I have a real bad feeling about this," Kendra said.

He nodded slowly. "There are hundreds of old vans in the Four Corners. Finding one based solely on the description we got is going to be tough."

"Even if we did, it doesn't mean the owner was driving it. It could have been stolen."

"Let's follow up on it from that angle, but meanwhile let's get out of this wind. I'll call Preston as we walk back to the truck and have him check the hot sheet. He'll put out a BOLO on the van, too," he said.

Paul brought out his phone but was forced to leave a voice mail.

Kendra's teeth were chattering by the time they got inside the truck. She wrapped Paul's leather jacket even more tightly around her and aimed the heating vent toward her. "Gusts like those get inside your clothing and chill you to the bone."

"The Navajo People say Wind's the messenger of the gods. Very little deters him."

"Is Wind supposed to bring good news or bad?" she asked.

"It brings…change."

"A nasty wind like this one, cold and bitter, can't bring anything good," she said, and shuddered, still cold.

"To those who'll remain outside, probably not. Be glad we'll have food to eat and a warm place to sleep tonight."

Again she heard that haunted tone in his voice. "You sound like someone who knows firsthand what it's like to be hungry and cold."

"I do. It happened to me more times than I care to remember."

She started to ask him more, but just then Paul's phone rang. It was Preston.

Kendra watched Paul, lost in thought. Before flying down to New Mexico she'd studied former Deputy U.S. Marshal Paul Grayhorse's file extensively. Yet the longer she was around him the more she realized that those cold facts didn't really tell Paul's story.

Paul glanced over at her as he was placed on hold. "Preston's checking the local and regional hot sheet. Let's see if he gets a hit on that van."

They didn't have long to wait, and with Preston's permission, Paul put him on speaker.

"Okay, here's what I got," Preston said. "We've had no reports of a stolen blue van in Hartley, but I broadened the search and found one in Durango, which is less than an hour away. The report is about two hours old, and, according to a witness, the van was last seen heading south."

"Toward New Mexico—and here," Paul said.

"So what are you thinking, bro?" Preston asked.

"Annie would have avoided 'Chuck' at all costs—unless he wore a disguise, which is one of Miller's areas of expertise," Paul said. "The fact that the john who picked her up had a beard and glasses…" He paused for a moment. "If we don't find Annie, she's as good as dead."

"I'll send additional units to the area, but we had a shooting outside a restaurant on the east side less than an hour ago. That gunman's still at large, so most of our available officers are there."

"Annie's an important witness," Paul said. "She's our only link to whoever's after me."

"I know, bro, but she's missing because she skipped out on our protection. We offered her a deal—we'd drop the B&E against her in exchange for her testimony and her ID'ing this 'Chuck' guy. Now that she's on the run, she'll lay low," Preston said. "I'll get a cruiser to work a grid pattern originating from the park, but for now that's all I can do."

After the call ended, Paul weighed their options. "I want to keep searching the area south of the bus depot for that van."

"Then let's do it."

Paul drove slowly around the old, run-down neighborhoods south of downtown. It was late. The few businesses around were closed, and most of the residences had only their porch lights on.

"The wind's really picked up," Kendra said as a hard gust slammed against the pickup. "I think we're in for snow."

He looked at the fast-moving, dark gray cloud bank low to the ground, coming in from the west. "The cold front is passing through, but all it'll bring will be blowing dust and virga—rain that never makes it to the ground. We're going into the third year of drought in New Mexico."

Paul hit three red lights in a row as he drove toward the old river bridge. As they approached the Turquoise Lights Motel, he slowed down and surveyed the parking lot.

"Over there, on the café side, by the trash bins," Kendra said, pointing.

Paul turned the truck around, then approached the big green Dumpsters. As he drew closer, a faded blue van became clearly visible in the floodlight mounted above a small loading dock. "It matches the description perfectly, down to the luggage rack and ladder in the back."

"We need to move in," Kendra said, reaching for her weapon. "Call for the closest backup."

"No," Paul said. "Let's not divert a unit unless we're sure. No one's visible in the van, and it's just sitting there with the driver's side window rolled down. Maybe it belongs to someone who works in the café. Let's go take a closer look."

"Okay, but be ready for surprises," she warned.

After parking so his own vehicle provided cover for them, Paul brought out his pistol.

"Let's go," he said.

Slipping around, he advanced from the rear of the van toward the passenger's side, his head low. If anyone raised up to look out, he'd see them in the side mirror.

Seconds later, he reached the window and looked inside. The keys were still in the ignition, but the bench-style backseat was empty.

"Clear in front," he called out.

Kendra was at the back of the vehicle, her weapon ready as Paul came around to join her.

Giving her a nod, Paul reached for the back handle and yanked it open. Kendra stepped up, her gun aimed at the interior.

"Crap." She lowered her weapon slowly. "We're too late."

Chapter Ten

Paul expelled his breath in a long hiss as he looked at Annie's lifeless body crumpled on the floor of the van. She was fully clothed, her hair in disarray. The loop of wire used to strangle her had cut deeply into Annie's neck, leaving a caked over pool of blood on the thinly carpeted floorboard.

"She hasn't been dead for long, and she fought him. See the defensive wounds on her arms?" Kendra said softly.

"I'll call it in." Paul spoke to his brother, then after about a minute, ended the call. "Preston told us to stay and protect the scene until officers arrive. After that, he needs us back at the station so he can take our statements."

"Better step back. We need to preserve the evidence," Kendra said.

He did as she'd asked. "We can still take a look from here," he said, then went back to his pickup and returned with a powerful flashlight. Standing about ten feet away, they both studied the interior.

"There's no blood splatter or scuff marks on the floorboard. He must have killed her outside the van, then tossed her into the back," Kendra said.

He turned off the light and stepped farther away. He was no Navajo Traditionalist, and he wasn't worried about the *chindi*, the evil in a man that was said to linger earthbound after death. Yet being around the dead still gave him the creeps.

Paul returned to his pickup with Kendra, then leaned back

against the cab watching the van. From here, neither of them could see the body, which was a good thing.

Kendra sighed. "Maybe she'll find peace now. The life she led must have been pure hell."

"When you have nothing, you have to fight to get out of that hole. If you don't, all you'll find is misery, or worse."

Kendra watched him closely for a while. He was all male, rugged and hard-muscled, yet his masculinity came with an amazing gentleness that could touch even the most jaded of hearts.

She tore her gaze away. "We need a new lead. Maybe in death, Annie will point the way. She's got the killer's DNA under her fingernails."

"We don't have Miller's DNA, or at least we didn't when I was in the marshals service," he said, looking at her.

"We still don't," she answered, "but this crime fits his profile. In a close-up kill, he likes getting his hands dirty."

Before he could comment, a patrol vehicle raced up. Behind it, halfway down the block, they could see the emergency lights of the crime scene van.

Kendra and Paul helped the officers secure the scene, then drove to the station.

Preston, who was talking to another detective in the area known as 'the bullpen,' saw them and waved. "My office, guys."

Kendra walked through the building, aware that she was under the scrutiny of every officer she passed. It was nothing unusual. No local law enforcement agency ever wanted a fed on their turf, especially a Deputy U.S. Marshal with jurisdiction virtually everywhere in the country.

"Don't let them psych you out," Paul said.

Surprised, she turned her head. She hadn't voiced the thought out loud, so she wasn't exactly sure what he was talking about. "What do you mean?"

"You're thinking the locals are giving you the usual mad-dogging stares reserved for feds, but that's not why they're looking at you," he said.

Just then Kendra reached the end of the hall. Preston waved her inside the open doorway.

"Take a seat," he said. "I'll be back in a minute. I need to talk to the captain."

Once they were alone and seated, Kendra answered Paul. "I'm used to getting some hostility from local departments. It goes with the job."

"They weren't sizing you up. They were checking you out, Kendra," he said with a smile. "Even wearing my clothes, you're a beautiful woman."

She was surprised by the impromptu compliment and his uncanny ability to read her. "You've got to tell me how you do that. I've never met anyone who can read people like you do. It's not just body language either. I know that already."

"It's Lynx."

"I don't know who or what Lynx is, but can I have some?"

He chuckled softly, but before he could say more, Preston walked back into the room.

"I need you both to make an official statement about what you saw at the murder scene. Paul, the desk sergeant in the bullpen will take yours. I'll handle Kendra's."

It was protocol to separate witnesses so they wouldn't influence each other's accounts, so this came as no surprise to her. "It'll go faster if you'll let me type out my statement," she said. "After you read it, I could also forward a copy to my supervisory inspector."

"Go for it," Preston said, waving her to his computer.

Kendra finished her report within five minutes. Preston then printed it out for her to sign.

"I'm sorry I don't have more to give you," she said.

"Our crime scene people are very good at their jobs, and they don't miss much. Even if this was the work of a pro, there may still be trace evidence we can use. Miller has a military record, so we can at least check for a blood type match."

Paul came in a moment later and took a seat. "Okay, that's done."

"Good. I've got some other news. The crime scene report on the incident over at Daniel's came in," Preston said. "The rounds came from a silenced thirty-two pistol. We found the casings. The defining thing is that while the shooter was positioned twenty yards away, he still came within a few inches of putting three rounds into your neck or skull. That indicates an incredible skill level, particularly with the subsonic rounds he was using."

"So this supports the theory that we're dealing with a pro," Kendra said.

"It's got to be Miller," Paul said. "High quality shooting like that requires extensive practice and training."

"There's also one big connection between the incident at Daniel's and what happened to Paul the night he went to meet Yolanda. Though different calibers were used, the rounds were all reloads, not factory made."

"So he has the foresight and ability to adapt his M.O.," Paul said.

Preston looked toward the door, where another detective was motioning to him. "Excuse me a moment," he said, getting up.

Now that they were alone again, Kendra stood, pushed her hands deep into her jacket pockets, and began to pace. Somewhere along the way, Chris Miller had managed to get inside her head. The truth was that he scared her in a way no other fugitive ever had.

Kendra straightened her back and forced herself to stand tall, her almost knee-jerk reaction to fear. She'd often been described as an exceptionally strong woman. Yet what the world defined as strength was simply her ability to bury raw emotions like fear deep inside herself in a place no one could see. For her, the cost of that had been loneliness. Not many understood that even the strongest woman could yearn to be held and comforted.

She walked to Preston's window, turning her back on Paul. She couldn't look him in the eyes right now. He saw way too much as it was. "I've been shot at before, Paul. It comes with the badge. But this man…"

"Drawing fire while trying to make an arrest is one thing, but being hunted—to be in a killer's crosshair—that's entirely different."

She turned around, but he'd come up from behind and she ended up bumping her nose against his chest.

He held his ground.

"How'd you get so close all of a sudden?" she muttered.

His nearness confused and excited her. Or maybe it was all a reaction to this case—knowing how close she'd come to death. All her senses were attuned to life and survival now.

"Could you step back just a little?" she said, forcing herself to meet his gaze.

He remained where he was. "I know what you're going through, Kendra. The knowledge that Miller, or whoever, wants you dead, is out there, waiting for his chance, is something that'll eat at you. What you need to do is make fear your ally. Use it to stay alert." He brushed his knuckles against the side of her face.

Maybe it was that gentle touch, or his tone of voice, or the way his eyes held hers, so steady, so sure. For whatever the reason, she didn't even bother hiding behind a string of denials. "I'm trained to hunt down fugitives—the worst of the worst—and I'm good at it. I do whatever has to be done. I shouldn't be feeling this way."

"Being tough doesn't mean we stop being human."

Hearing footsteps, Paul moved away, giving her space.

Kendra dropped back down into her chair just as Preston came into the room.

"Annie's body showed no signs of livor mortis, that darkening of the skin where the blood pools, so she'd been dead less than a half hour when you found her. That fresh a crime scene may give us some answers."

"Did the motel or restaurant have a surveillance system?" Kendra asked.

"Only inside at the front desk and cash registers," Preston said.

A short time later they walked back to Paul's truck. "You're a mass of compressed energy and tension right now, Kendra. You need to work some of that off so you can think clearly again. So tell me, when you're off duty, how do you deal with this? The gym?"

"No, I jog," she said.

"Okay, so how about going for a run with me right now? The wind's died down."

"It's close to midnight," she answered. "Where can we find a track that's not going to turn us into instant targets?"

"What I have in mind isn't a track, not exactly anyway. It's a beautiful trail, particularly by moonlight."

"Sounds like you've done this before."

He nodded. "There are times when running is the only thing that can help take my mind off things. When I'm running, the only thing I think about is my next step."

"Me, too," she said. "So stop someplace where I can pick up some gear. I can't run in these clothes."

"Hartley has an all-night MallMart. You can get some sweats there. As for me, I'm covered. I've got stuff in the back of the cab. If I ever want to go somewhere on the spur of the moment, I can."

"And that includes running shoes and stuff?" she asked, surprised.

He laughed. "I keep a little of everything with me. I don't like doing without."

It was the way he'd said it that made a million questions

pop into her head. Maybe, while they were jogging, she'd get him to talk about himself. Then again, maybe it would take everything she had just to stay even with him.

Chapter Eleven

Some time later they pulled into an empty parking area next to the *bosque,* the wooded area flanking the river. "We're way past their posted hours," Kendra said, a trace of disappointment in her voice.

"No one will bother us. I know the park staff and they know me." He climbed out of the pickup, placing his weapon and other essentials inside the front pockets of his hooded sweatshirt.

As he stepped toward the trailhead she became delightfully aware of the way his sweats accentuated his height and hard muscles. She didn't know if he had gym shorts on beneath or not, but either way he had the best butt she'd ever seen. She bit back a sigh.

He looked over at her and grinned. "Window shopping?"

"I wasn't...."

He grinned even wider.

"I'm here for the run. I need to wind down," she said.

"Exercise? There are other ways...."

"Not for me," she snapped, wishing again things could have been different. "When I'm working, I don't like distractions." She'd said it more for her own benefit than for his.

"Sometimes I think you're wrapped way too tight."

"You think too much," she countered, then took off at a fast clip, hurdling the low metal gate designed to keep vehicle traffic off the foot trail.

He caught up easily in a few seconds, laughing. "I *think* too much?"

She increased her speed, though it was tough going on that winding cobblestone trail, and evened her breathing. She intended to jog at least an hour. Unless she was close to exhaustion by the time they finished, she wouldn't be able to sleep tonight.

After ten minutes she realized that she was setting the pace. "Am I going too fast?"

"Not at all. I'm just enjoying the view from back here."

She slowed down immediately. "Why don't we run side by side…unless you want to drop out now," she added, immediately contrite. "I have no idea what kind of rehab program you're following."

"Why are you worried?" He came up beside her, his voice not at all winded. "Do I look out of shape?"

She didn't have to glance over to answer. "Far from it."

"Then don't worry about me. Choose whatever pace you're used to following. I'll keep up."

"I run three or four hours a week," she said.

"So it's not that far then."

Now she'd done it. Her competitive nature would never let her quit first—and clearly neither would his.

After another half hour, halfway around the big loop that wound up and down both banks of the cold river, she glanced over at Paul. To her annoyance, he wasn't even breathing hard.

"You look as if we've been out on a stroll, not running up and down these inclines. That's some stamina," she said.

"When I was living on the Rez my brothers and I would race each other up and down the canyon trails. It was a great way to work off excess energy and stay fit. The closest gym was at the high school, and that was thirty miles away. Most of the time we didn't have the gas money for trips like that, so we worked out at home."

"You mentioned that sometimes you were completely broke

and had to go hungry," she said, hoping he'd talk about himself a bit more.

"That was before the foster homes, and before I went to live with *Hosteen* Silver."

"Life must have been tough when you were a kid." She slowed down without even realizing it, more interested in their conversation than in jogging.

"I guess. My mom did her best, but she was barely sixteen when she got pregnant. She quit high school to have me, so she never graduated. She took whatever jobs she could find, kitchen help, cleaning, stuff like that. By the time I turned eight she just gave up. I think she was ill, cancer or something like that. One day she dropped me off at a fire station, and I never saw her again. New Mexico Children, Youth and Families Department took custody after that."

He'd been matter-of-fact, and the only indication that the past still caused him pain was that he'd increased his pace, as if he were trying to outrun the memory.

"Eight years old is so young," she said, trying to keep up with him. She wouldn't offer him sympathy she knew he didn't want, but she could show him support by just staying beside him. "Did you know at the time that she wouldn't be coming back?"

"No. We'd taken the bus, and when she dropped me off, she handed me a sealed envelope. I was supposed to give it to the first fireman I saw. Later I found out it was a letter relinquishing custody of me. For a long time, I kept thinking she'd come back for me after she got better. It never happened."

"Did you ever find out what happened to her?" she asked, increasing her pace to match his.

"Not for years. I figured since she'd thrown me away, there was nothing for me to find." He slowed down, and their pace returned to a fast jog. "Eventually I found out that she passed away about six months after she left me at the fire station."

Although Paul's words held no trace of emotion, the revelation stunned her. She'd known about the wound on his shoulder, but the scars he bore inside went far deeper than any bullet ever could.

Somehow the moon, the darkness and the physical exertion had worked a magic all their own and helped her see a side of him she doubted many ever saw.

"It's a beautiful night. Let's just enjoy the moonlight for a while," she said, slowing down to a walk.

"Tired?"

"Me? No, not at all," she said, unwilling to admit it. Realizing he was going to speed up again, she bit back a groan. "Slow down anyway. I'm tired of being in a hurry. The pressure to get there first is part of everything I seem to be doing lately."

"I get that," he said, and slowed to a walk. "The urge to see the payoff at the end of the line is always there. It can make the journey nothing short of a test of endurance."

"Yeah, it feels like that sometimes. Even in my private life I'm always racing to reach a new goal."

"Like what?" His voice was softer now, gentle.

"I've been looking into adoption," she said, liking the way he'd stepped closer to her. She could feel the warmth of his body wrapping itself around her, and the way he was looking at her made her tingle all the way down to her toes.

She looked away and struggled to clear her thinking. "There are some holdbacks I've yet to work out, but I'm not giving up on the idea."

"Why not just have a baby of your own?"

To her credit, she didn't sigh, but it took a concerted effort not to look at him. "I've considered that, but, to me, adoption is the way to go."

"How come?"

"It's complicated," she said.

"We've got time." Seeing her hesitate, he added, "We need to get to know each other, Kendra. Working as partners, even for who knows how long, means we have to learn to trust each other all the way. I don't like talking about my past, but I've told you a little about myself. Now it's your turn. Help us maintain the balance between us. By doing that, you'll also be honoring Navajo ways."

"All right," she said after a moment. "It all goes back to the days where 'home' was wherever the colonel's change of station took us. We traveled all over the world. One of the things I learned back then was that in an amazing number of countries poor kids have no chance, no future. Toddlers and their mothers would be living on the streets, and older kids sometimes completely on their own."

She paused, then in a soft voice, continued. "I know I can't change the world, but maybe I can make a difference in one life. International adoptions are complicated, but someday that's what I'd like to do."

"There are kids in our own country who could use a loving home. Look at my brothers and me. *Hosteen* Silver changed our lives. He gave us a future."

"I know," she said quietly, "but in the U.S. babies and toddlers are harder to find, and preference is usually given to two-parent homes."

"You're not planning to marry?"

"It's not that I've ruled it out, but there's no man in my life and I don't know if there ever will be," she said. "A single-parent adoption, particularly for someone in my profession, is difficult. I've got practically no chance in the U.S."

"Yeah, running down fugitives, transporting prisoners, and having to travel halfway across the country at a moment's notice could be real tough for a single parent."

"I've taken all that into account myself. That's one of the reasons I haven't gone any further than fact-finding. I have a lot of things to work out first."

Aware of how much she'd revealed about herself, she suddenly grew quiet. It had been way too easy to open up to Paul.

His nearness, the sound of his low, sexy voice, and the quiet beauty of the *bosque* trail had conspired against her.

Soon after they'd rounded a curve in the trail, the *bosque* became increasingly dense. She picked up the pace. "We're hemmed in here, and I can't see into the trees. Tactically, this isn't a good place for us."

She'd barely finished speaking when they both heard a deep catlike growl coming from the brush to the right of the cobblestone path. All she could see was a dark shape and two amber eyes gleaming in the moonlight.

Kendra reached for her gun slowly, glad she always carried her weapon, even when off duty. If the animal attacked she'd be able to defend Paul and herself.

"Don't. We're in no danger," he said in a barely audible voice.

"It's a wildcat and it's coming toward us."

"It won't harm us."

Paul stepped in front of Kendra and pulled out the leather cord he wore around his neck. Something hung from it, but she couldn't make out what it was. A good luck charm? She preferred bullets. Her gaze shifted back to what appeared to be a bobcat that was advancing silently toward them with graceful but deliberate strides.

Paul took another step toward it, effectively blocking the creature's path. "Go your way and walk in beauty, my brother."

Kendra kept her hand on the grip of her pistol, but, to her surprise, the animal stopped its advance. It seemed to nod, though it was probably just a twitch, then turned away and walked off into the undergrowth.

It wasn't until the cat had disappeared completely that she finally drew in a full breath. "Guess we're too big to take on."

"That wasn't it. He never intended to attack. The cat came out to honor the connection between him and me. The animal kingdom is more attuned to things like that than the Anglo world is." Paul fell into step beside her. "What amazes me is that he approached even though there were two of us."

"I don't understand what you mean when you say you two are connected. Do you think the cat saw you as a friend?"

"No, not exactly. It's more, and less, than that." He took off the leather cord from around his neck and showed her the small fetish that hung from it. "It's a lynx, carved from oak. *Hosteen* Silver gave it to me right before I left to join the marshals service. Although all my brothers had their fetishes given to them on or around their sixteenth birthday, mine remained uncarved until that day."

"Was he punishing you for something?" They were walking side by side now, close enough to touch, but not doing so despite the temptation.

"No, not punishing—teaching. You see, I'd always played things close to my chest, and I guess that made me hard to read. On my sixteenth birthday he told me that I was still a work in progress. Until I became the man I was meant to be, he couldn't be sure which fetish would be the right spiritual match for me. Then, a few days before I was scheduled to report to the USMS training academy in Georgia, *Hosteen* Silver had a very vivid dream. He told me about it. He said he saw a beautiful lynx walking ahead of me as we went out on a hunt, so *Hosteen* Silver honored the sign and had the carving made for me from this piece of oak. I've worn it ever since, and as *Hosteen* Silver promised, it's proven to be invaluable."

"How so?" she asked. Paul's voice drew her. She wanted to stop, hold the fetish…and him.

"It's said that each fetish possesses the qualities of the animal it represents and shares them with its owner," Paul said, slipping the fetish around his neck again. "Lynx knows what others try to keep secret, and sees what's not readily apparent. That's why Lynx is the perfect match for someone in our profession. We have to find the truth, no matter how deeply it's hidden. We're also hunters."

"Maybe *I* should carry a lynx fetish," she said. "Do you think it would work for me?"

He shook his head. "Lynx isn't the right match for you. One of the things Lynx does is bring you knowledge that you may have forgotten about yourself. But you have no hidden past, as far as I can tell."

"No, I don't."

"I'll tell you what, then. Give me a chance to think this over, and as I get to know you better, I'll find the right fetish animal match for you," he said as they reached the end of the trail.

"Remind me never to say no to a run with you," she said walking with him to his truck. "It's been an amazing night."

"What still surprises me is that the cat allowed you to see him. That's not the way it normally works. I wonder what he was trying to tell me." Looking into her eyes, Paul stepped closer to her. "What does he know about you that I don't, Kendra?"

Everything about him enticed her and teased her senses. The fire in his eyes called to her, whispering temptation. More than anything, she wanted to feel his arms around her, to rest against his chest and enjoy the heat there.

He tilted her chin upwards, ready to cover her mouth with his.

Suddenly his cell phone rang, startling both of them.

Paul cursed, moved back a few steps, and glanced at the caller ID. "It's Preston," he growled.

While Paul spoke to his brother, she took a deep breath. Her body was still tingling and not from the cold. She sighed softly as she looked at Paul, wondering what his kiss would have been like. Would he have been tender at first, then rough? Would he have deepened his kiss slowly or would it have started that way?

She swallowed hard and looked at her surroundings for a moment. She had to keep her mind off Paul and on business.

"I have no idea where we'll sleep tonight," Paul was saying to Preston, "but it won't be Copper Canyon. Things are happening here, so this is where we have to be, close to the action."

The realization that, in order to stay alive, they'd have to spend the night standing guard over each other put her thoughts back on track. What had she been thinking? If there was ever a time *not* to let her guard down, this was it.

Paul hung up and glanced at her. "My brother suggested a motel that's not too far from here. The owner is an ex-cop, and the local D.A. occasionally uses the place to sequester a jury or hide away a key witness."

"Sounds good to me," she said.

He brought out his truck keys and opened the doors with the remote. "You and I are up against a pro who's getting paid for the hit. He won't give up till it's done."

As she looked into Paul's eyes, she saw a renewed sense of caution mirrored there. As much as she wanted to prolong this tender moment with him, living to take their next breath had to take priority now.

Chapter Twelve

The Blue Mountain Lodge, a long, cinder block rectangular building with thirty guest rooms, stood at the edge of town. It backed up against a six foot concrete wall and could only be approached from the front and sides. It also faced a fairly busy street.

"The local cops like this place because of the layout," he said. "The halls are covered by security cameras. One of the exterior doors is next to the front desk, and the other is an emergency exit with an alarm. That one's always locked on the outside after nine pm. The halls are ceramic tile, too, so the sound of footsteps carries a long way."

"Good," she said, stifling a yawn. "I'm beat, Paul, so how would you feel about taking the first watch tonight? Unless I get a few hours of sleep, I may not be able to stay alert."

"No problem. I'm not ready for sleep yet, so I'll keep a lookout."

Paul parked on the side of the building next to the main entrance. To his right was a small, attached restaurant.

As they passed through a small glass-walled foyer and entered the lobby where the main desk was located, the husky man behind the counter grinned. "Hey, Grayhorse, how you doing?"

"Jimmy Masters? I thought you were still on the force." Paul stepped forward, bumped fists with the man, then turned around and introduced Kendra. "Jimbo and I went to high school together."

Kendra shook hands with him. Jimmy had blue eyes and dark hair. He was about twenty pounds or so overweight, but he still seemed way too young for retirement.

"I took a fall chasing a suspect and trashed my knee. After that I couldn't pass the physical. The department couldn't find me a desk job because of the economy, so here I am," he said, answering their unspoken question.

"That's a tough break, man. I'm sorry," Paul said.

"It's not so bad. I work nights and my wife days, so there's always someone home with the kids, and we have our weekends together. We're doing good."

"I'm glad you made things work," Paul said.

"Word is you're in a bit of trouble," Jimmy said. "I spoke to Preston a while ago, and he filled me in, so I got you a room halfway down the hall on the right. With the emergency door secured from the inside, the only way anyone can approach is to walk past this desk or break in the window. The curtains are also thick enough to keep anyone from tracking you from the outside. So no worries there."

"Thanks. That'll make things easier," Kendra said.

"I also put an extra carafe of coffee in your room, and some snacks in case you get hungry."

"We appreciate it, Jimbo," Paul said. "Mind if I take a quick look at your surveillance coverage?"

"No prob." Jimmy gestured to a small room just beyond the open doorway behind him. "We have very few late night drop-in guests this time of the year, so I'll be able to spot any activity right away."

Paul went in, looked around, then gave Kendra a nod.

"Okay then, we're good," Kendra said.

As they walked down the hall to their room, Paul gave her a quick half grin. "Good thing we're both beat. It'll keep us out of trouble."

She took a deep breath. "Paul, about what happened earlier…"

"I already know what you're going to say and you're right. We're working a case where one slipup could get us both killed. We can't afford to get sidetracked. Maybe after it's all said and done…"

She didn't answer. There was no need. It was clear to both of them that she was here to do a job. Afterwards, she'd go back to her life, and he, to his. If she could somehow manage to keep that firmly in mind, she'd be fine.

Paul opened the door and Kendra stepped into the room. Only one bed. It was as if fate itself was determined to tempt them. "We'll take turns keeping watch. Are you sure you're okay taking the first shift?"

"Absolutely," Paul answered.

"If you leave the room to catch up on old times with your friend, don't feel like you have to wake me. I really need some sleep and this is a secure location."

"No prob," he said.

Kendra went to the bed, pulled down the covers and, after kicking off her shoes, crawled in. The warmth and the weight of the blankets did the job, and she drifted off to sleep.

As her mind opened to the dreamscape before her, Kendra found herself on a hunt with a man couched in shadows, while the cries of a wildcat echoed through the darkness.

It was 3:00 a.m., according to the digital clock on the nightstand.

Paul watched Kendra sleep, glad to see her looking at peace. As she smiled and shifted her hips, he wondered what she was dreaming about and if he'd come to visit her there. The possibility played on in his imagination, making him hard.

Expelling his breath in a hiss, Paul looked away and stood to stretch his legs. As he did, he spotted the flashing light on their room phone. He picked it up instantly, before it had a chance to ring.

"Paul, it's me," Jim said quickly. "I'm not sure if what I've got is important, but I thought I'd pass the information along. About a half hour ago, a dark-colored pickup parked outside for several minutes, then drove away. It's back again, and it's now parked on the south side between the Dumpsters. I think he's talking on his cell phone. Do you want me to call Preston and have him send over an officer?"

"No, let me check it out first," Paul said, speaking in a whisper. "I don't see how anyone could have tracked us here."

Paul watched Kendra for a moment, listening to the even sound of her breathing. Last time he'd stepped away without waking her, she'd pulled a gun on him, mistaking him for an intruder. She'd told him that she slept light, but not tonight. The jog had done its job, allowing her to sleep soundly. She hadn't woken up despite his brief conversation.

He slipped out of the room quietly. He didn't need backup at this point, and Jimbo was keeping watch and would alert her, if needed.

The moment he was out in the hall, he used his cell phone to call Jim. "Keep a close eye on the hall and make sure no one approaches our door. While my partner's sleeping I'm going to take a quick look around. If I get any bad vibes, I'll call in the cavalry."

"Copy that," Jimmy said, his tone reverting to that of the officer he'd been once.

Paul was only a few steps from the lobby when he heard footsteps ahead. It was Jimmy, coming around the front desk.

"I'll cover the hall," he said softly, giving Paul a nod.

As Paul slipped outside, the cold air cut into him like an icy blade. He hadn't worn his jacket, wanting ease of movement and free access to his holstered weapon.

Walking quietly down the sidewalk, he passed the restaurant, now dark and silent. Once he reached the corner, Paul

stopped and looked out toward the Dumpsters, which were positioned about fifty feet down the six foot high concrete wall.

Between the two big trash bins he could see the tail end of a
solitary pickup. The driver had parked at an angle so he could
have a clear view of the main entrance and front corner of the
building. It was a method someone with training in surveillance techniques would have used. The position concealed the
driver's face and intentions while allowing him to utilize his
side and rearview mirrors to give him an unobstructed view.

The cloud of water vapor escaping from the truck's tailpipe
told Paul the engine was on, so the driver was undoubtedly
inside. He decided to move in for a closer look.

As he inched toward the wall, screening himself with the
large trash containers that also hid the pickup, he heard light
footsteps coming up from behind.

Paul turned in a crouch, pistol in hand.

"It's me," Kendra whispered. "Jim said you'd be here checking out some pickup."

"You were sound asleep when I left. What woke you?"

"Jimmy's footsteps. Then he dropped his keys. I looked
though the peephole, ID'd him, and got the story. Is that the
pickup behind the trash bins?" she whispered.

He nodded. "The way he's screening himself and the fact
that he's come and gone once already…"

Kendra nodded. "Let's go check it out. Split up. I'll go
right, you go left."

"No, let's advance along this wall using the Dumpsters for
cover. If it's our guy, he'll be packing," Paul said.

"Bad plan," she said. "If he has a gun, he won't show it till
you're at point-blank range. I won't see it either, not in time
to back you up. Or he'll just shoot through the door and you'll
never see it coming. Let me angle back, circle the motel, and
come in from his passenger's side blind spot. There's no way
he can cover both flanks."

"Go." Paul reached the shoulder-high trash bin, weapon

pointed down, and waited until he could see Kendra at the far corner of the motel. Moving quickly, he walked toward the driver's window, and as he closed in, he studied the driver's profile. He was sitting back in his seat, still unaware of their presence.

Kendra continued her approach from the right and was less than fifty feet away when the driver inside the truck turned his head toward the side mirror and spotted Kendra.

"U.S. Marshal!" Kendra yelled, crouching on one knee and bringing up her pistol. "Show me your hands!"

The driver instantly threw the pickup into reverse, spinning the steering wheel and racing backwards straight toward her.

"Bail," Paul yelled, pointing toward the Dumpster.

Kendra raced him to their only refuge, diving just ahead of him into the trash bin.

They landed on top of a section of flattened cardboard just as the pickup bounced off the metal corner. They were tossed around between trash filled bags but avoided the sheet metal sides. Before either of them could regain their balance, they heard the pickup race away, tires squealing.

"He's gone," Kendra said, pushing aside a trash bag. She tried to take a step but slipped and fell onto her hands and knees. "What is that smell?"

Paul made it to the edge and hoisted himself up and out. "I think it's a skunk," he said, grabbing Kendra's hands and helping her climb out.

"You okay?" Paul asked, taking short breaths and fighting to keep from gagging.

"That stench just rips the air out of your lungs," she said, coughing.

"We need to shower and change. Once we can breathe again, we'll sort things out," Paul said.

Jim ran to meet them. "I saw what—" He suddenly turned his face away and covered his mouth and nose with one hand. "You found the skunk."

"Yeah, seems so," Paul said.

Jim took another step back. "It wandered onto the parking lot just after dark and got run over. The restaurant manager had one of his people put it into a plastic bag and toss it in there. You must have ripped open the bag when you went Dumpster diving."

"Lucky us," Paul said.

Jim curled his nose. "You're going to need my special mixture. It's dry mustard and a few other choice ingredients." He glanced at Paul. "Works fast. You might want to shower together so the scent won't spread to the curtains and bedding."

Paul glanced at Kendra and grinned. "Hey, it's our duty to step up in an emergency."

"In your dreams," she shot back. Not that she would have minded. The thought of seeing him naked under a hot spray in the shower left her tingling all over. "No showering together, and it's too cold to hose off outside. What's plan B?" she said as they approached the main entrance.

"Paul, shower in the first room on the right. Kendra, take the one on the left. I'll let you in, then bring you both some odor remover and plastic bags for your clothing. And work fast, will you? Otherwise I'll never get that scent out of the hall—or the rooms. It'll get on everything."

"If we're in the shower, someone will have to stand guard out in the hall," Paul said.

"I'll do it. I've got a concealed carry permit and my .38," he said, lifting his jacket. "Just wait in the foyer for a sec, okay?"

"Go get the stuff," Kendra said.

It took Kendra a full twenty minutes before she felt clean enough to finally step out of the shower. She'd used the descenter and the perfumed soap and had washed her hair several times.

Since she hadn't wanted to handle anything until she'd rid herself of that awful skunk smell, she hadn't brought a change of clothes into the bathroom. Taking one of the large, plush towels, she wrapped it around herself and stepped into the room.

To her surprise, Paul was there. She stopped in midstride and stared at him, unable to tear her gaze away from his loose, open shirt. She'd never seen that much of his bare chest before, and it was a sight to behold. He had the perfect build. From what she could see, he had just the right amount of muscle for her tastes and a flat stomach that rippled with raw masculine strength. Low-slung jeans sparked her imagination even more, making her wish she could see the rest. Soon her fingertips tingled with the need to touch him.

Using all her willpower, she looked away. That's when she saw the first aid kit on the table beside him. "Are you hurt?" she asked quickly.

"I got a few cuts and scratches from those big staples on the cardboard box. Do you have any scrapes that need tending? I'd be happy to put on the antiseptic." His gaze traveled over her like a slow, intimate caress.

"I need my clothes," she managed in a hoarse voice, suddenly remembering that her carry-on was still in Paul's truck.

"Jimbo brought in your things while you were in the shower. You'll find everything in the closet."

She hurried to her small suitcase, started to bend over, then abruptly changed her mind. "You can either get out of the room, or put the bag on the bed for me."

"How about if I put you on the bed first and check you over for cuts?" he said, his eyes never leaving hers. "I promise to be thorough."

Her breath caught in her throat, and her heart began to pound so loudly she was sure he'd hear it. "We're in trouble, Paul. Try to act like it."

He gave her a heart-stopping grin. "We're not in trouble… not yet."

To her own credit, she managed an icy glare. "I'm going

back into the bathroom to get dressed," she said, bending at the knees and grabbing a handful of clothes. "Afterwards, we'll discuss what happened and figure out what's next."

Kendra dressed quickly. Slacks, a plain navy blue pullover sweater and a dark blazer were practically a uniform for her these days. She chose them now, hoping to remind herself that she was never off the clock when working a case like this one.

When she went back out into the room, Paul still had his shirt open. Those low-slung jeans seemed to fit even lower on his hips now, or maybe that was just her imagination.

"You planning to finish getting dressed soon?"

"I'm decent—or am I distracting you?" He gave her a slow, devastating grin.

"No, you're annoying me." Paul was relentless when he wanted something, and at the moment he appeared to want her. The knowledge thrilled her and made her ache for things she had no business wanting.

"You're not being truthful with me or yourself," he said, taking a step closer.

She held her ground, refusing to back away. "You're used to getting your way with women, Paul, but I'm out of your reach."

"Not at all," he murmured, the warmth of his breath almost touching her lips.

She stepped around him and gathered her things. "Paul, I came to New Mexico to do a job. That, and staying alive, are my only priorities."

"Life is short. Enjoying special moments is sometimes all we've got," he said. "Don't pass them up."

She heard the dark undertone woven through his words. His past was marked by the loss of people who'd mattered to him. Although she understood what drove Paul, she lived her life by a different set of rules. "I'm not your type, Paul. I want a lot more from a guy than a good time in bed. It may sound old-fashioned, but there it is."

"So you're looking for your forever guy?"

"I'm not really sure there's such a thing, at least for me, but without something solid to back it up, physical attraction fades away. I want the whole package, not just pieces of it."

"You might end up taking on more than you can handle."

"As I see it, the real danger is settling for something less." She said it firmly, needing to believe it, but Paul had awakened a new yearning inside her. It remained deep inside her heart—a temptation couched in two simple words— "what if."

Chapter Thirteen

They'd returned to their original room, and now it was Kendra's turn to watch Paul sleep. She'd had to insist that he try to get some rest. Finally, after tossing and turning for a long time, he seemed to have drifted off.

Kendra sat next to the small table at one end of the room, staring at the latest issue of *New Mexico Magazine*. On the cover was a photo of children playing in front of a picturesque *casita*.

She sighed softly. As much as she loved the marshals service, she knew the job would make it almost impossible for her to become a single mom. Yet investigative work was what she did best. She'd considered working in the private sector, but no job in her field would ever come with a guarantee of regular hours. She'd also need a decent paycheck that included good benefits. Without all that, she still wouldn't be able to qualify as an adoptive parent.

The obstacles that stood in her way seemed insurmountable. Maybe some dreams weren't meant to be.

As she leaned back and stretched, she heard soft, padding footsteps in the hallway. She went to the door, her hand on the grip of her pistol.

Kendra listened carefully and heard what sounded like a scratching sound near the electronic lock. Maybe it was nothing, housekeeping or an inebriated motel guest, but too much had happened already for her to ignore it.

"Paul!" she whispered harshly.

He was up instantly, and from her position near the door, he seemed to figure out the rest.

"Throw it open," he said, his words barely audible. "I'll handle it." He flattened against the other side of the door.

Kendra slipped off the security chain, then held up one finger, then two. There was no three. In a lightning fast move, she pulled the door open.

Paul yanked the man into the room and threw him down onto the floor. Kendra moved in, her weapon aimed at his chest.

It was Preston. Kendra immediately lowered her weapon.

"What the hell do you think you're doing, creeping around out there, bro?" Paul demanded, offering his brother a hand up. "You have a death wish?"

"You never sleep, so I figured you'd be the one keeping watch. I used our signal."

"Signal? I didn't hear anything except footsteps and an odd scratching sound," she said.

"*That's* the signal," Preston said. "It was something we came up with back home whenever we wanted to sneak out of the house. Whoever stayed behind was supposed to cover for the other one. We had different rooms and if we'd gotten together to make plans, *Hosteen* Silver would have heard us."

"I think he knew and just chose to ignore it," Paul said.

Preston chuckled. "I came up with that particular signal because it sounds like a cat scratching, and Paul's like a stray with nine lives. The son of a gun lands on his feet no matter how many times you toss him across the room."

Paul laughed. "When was the last time you could do that?"

"Have you had these selective memory problems long?" Preston countered without missing a beat.

"Guys," she said, interrupting them. "Preston, I assume you're here for a reason. Has something new turned up?"

"Yeah," he said. "I paid John Lucas a visit this morning and my hunch paid off."

"I don't know the name," Kendra said.

"Lucas owns a gun shop and a very popular shooting range just outside the city limits," Preston said. "The rounds that were used against both of you were hand cast from linotype, so I figured the gunman might want to purchase additional supplies soon. Lucas is the only local source of metal for cast bullets."

"John's pretty closed-mouthed, particularly around cops. How did you persuade him to loosen up?" Paul asked.

"Enlightened self-interest," he said, not elaborating. "He told me to speak to Gil Davies. He said that if there was out-of-town talent working here, Gil would know."

"I've heard the name, but I can't place the guy," Paul said.

"He runs a survivalist training camp. He's also suspected of dealing black market guns, but no one's ever been able to get any evidence to back that up. What we've got is more rumor and gossip than anything, but I trust my informant. If he says Davies is the man to talk to, you can count on it. The problem is that Davies is out of my jurisdiction. You'll need to talk to him, Kendra."

"Where exactly do I find this Gil Davies?" Kendra asked.

"He has a small place just off Highway 145 north of Cortez, Colorado, about fifteen miles from my brother Gene's ranch. I've been told he's not friendly to uninvited guests, so watch your backs. You're more likely to be greeted with firearms than open arms."

Kendra glanced at Paul, and for the first time found she could read what was going on in his head. She recognized the signs—that initial rush of adrenaline, mingled with iron-willed control. It was the latter that he'd draw on to exercise restraint.

"You know where we're headed, right?" she asked Paul.

"Yeah, no problem. It's a little over an hour from here. Nine-thirty now, we'll get there by ten-thirty."

"Okay. Let's go," she said.

"Stay alert for surprises," Preston said as they walked out. "There's nothing but empty highway once you pass through Shiprock and turn north."

"We'll handle it," Kendra said, acutely aware of the weight of the badge on her belt.

A HALF HOUR later, beyond the reservation town of Shiprock, the road stretching north before them seemed endless. She shifted in her seat, absently noting the series of tower-like mesas to the east.

"Restless?" he asked.

"Yeah, the scenery is beautiful, but I need something to focus on. How about going over some contingency plans?"

Paul shook his head. "Planning every detail is just a way of fooling yourself into thinking you have control over the situation. That false sense of security can be dangerous."

"If you plan for the most likely eventualities, you have a better chance of achieving your objectives," she said.

He smiled at her. "That sounds like something the colonel taught you."

She laughed. "It is. The colonel always got things done, and he expected the same from my brother and me. He taught us independence and responsibility, and never tolerated excuses of any kind."

"You've barely mentioned your brother. I gather you two aren't that close?" he asked.

"No, we're not. In the colonel's household we looked out for ourselves and learned not to ask for help. He expected us to be leaders, not followers, so depending on someone else was considered a sign of weakness."

"So, you and your brother each went your own way?"

"Exactly." She smiled. "I know you're close to your brothers, but Gene went his own way, chose ranching instead of law enforcement. Does he still belong to the pack?"

He nodded. "Yeah, we're all there for each other anytime, no matter what. But you're right. Gene's always marched to his own drummer." He paused, collecting his thoughts. "The guy was practically born to be a rancher. He has an amazing way with animals, particularly horses."

"And you don't?" she asked, sensing what he'd left unsaid.

"That's the understatement of the year," Paul said with a wry grin. "That's why it made no sense when *Hosteen* Silver left his horse to me instead of Gene. His last request was that I learn to be friends with Grit."

"You own a horse!" she said, enthusiasm evident in her tone.

He smiled. "You like horses?"

"I love them, but excuse me for interrupting your story. Tell me more about Grit. Why is it difficult for you two to become friends?"

"There's really no story. We're not friends because, basically, the horse hates me. To date, he's never let me ride him. Every time I've tried I've ended up facedown in the dirt. I was the one who named him Grit because that's what ended up in my mouth each time I was tossed," he said, laughing. "I've done everything I can think of to get on better terms with that animal, but Grit's not interested."

"Maybe you're trying too hard," she said.

He looked at her in surprise. "That's exactly what Gene says, but I'd like to get this over with as soon as possible. It's important."

"I don't follow," she said.

"It's part of the puzzle *Hosteen* Silver left for me." A minute or two stretched out as he tried to decide how much to tell her. Kendra had a sharp mind and investigative training. The fact that she wasn't directly involved might mean she'd be able to offer him new insights on *Hosteen* Silver's letter. "I could really use your take on something, but it involves family business, so it would have to stay between us."

"I can keep a secret when it's not case related, and I enjoy working with puzzles. I'd love to help, if I can."

"I've already told you a little about *Hosteen* Silver and the kind of man he was. After he passed away, we discovered that he'd left each of us a letter. The ones that have been opened so far have contained both a prediction and a final request. What he asked of me was that I become friends with his horse. That also plays a part in what he foretold for me." Seeing the questions in her eyes, he gave her a shortened version. "He said that enemies would become friends, and friends enemies, but Grit would show me the way, *if* I became his friend."

"Maybe that was his way of making sure Grit would always be looked after," she said.

Paul shook his head. "The horse was already in good hands living at my brother Gene's ranch. Had he asked Gene, it would have made perfect sense, but he asked *me*. Gene thinks maybe *Hosteen* Silver wanted me to learn patience, but I don't buy it. As an investigator, I've already got more than my share of that."

"And the horse has always given you problems?"

"From the very beginning," Paul said, nodding. "I tried to befriend him lots of times, but he's never been interested."

"I'm not an expert, but I know a little about horses. They can kick, buck and bite if you make them angry enough. Maybe the lesson wasn't about patience as much as it was about not trying to force certain things." She paused and took a breath. "What do you think? Does that sound like him?"

He considered it for a moment, then nodded slowly. "Yeah, it does. When I look at Grit, I see an animal I'm going to have to outlast, intimidate or fight, and that affects how I deal with him," he said with a wry smile. "Thanks for your insight, Kendra. Figuring out what *Hosteen* Silver was really trying to say has never been easy for any of us."

"Thanks for letting me help."

A half hour later they drove up a long, narrow dirt road in southwestern Colorado's ranching country. At the end of their bumpy ride they found a closed metal gate with a sign that read Last Stand Ranch. No Trespassing.

"It's closed but not locked," she said. "Maybe he's expecting a delivery."

"Once he sees us, he'll be mighty disappointed."

"Let's drive in and find out, but let me lead. I'm not so threatening."

A ghost of a smile tugged at the corners of his mouth. "And you think I am?"

"It's the package. You seem to know how to work it." Biting back a smile, she didn't give him time to answer. "Let's roll."

Chapter Fourteen

The road just beyond the gate was so rutted it took them nearly five minutes to reach the freshly painted, white wood framed house. About fifty yards to its left stood a classic bright red barn. Paul parked next to a utility pole off to the side of the main house.

"Quiet and peaceful, not my vision of a survivalist's home," Kendra said after exiting the pickup. She checked the position of her weapon. "Let me take point. I'd like him to assume we're a couple who got lost. Once we're face-to-face and he can see my weapon, I'll identify myself."

As he got out of the pickup, Paul looked around. His fetish felt heavy, a sure sign that something wasn't quite right.

"Something feels…wrong." He held up his hand, asking for quiet. In the distance was the rumbling sound of metal clinking and clacking. "Reloading equipment—one of those vibrating case cleaners," he said, then gestured to the barn.

"If he's over there processing some ammo, that might explain why he didn't hear us drive up," she said. "Let's check out the barn first."

Paul hung back like she'd asked, his gaze taking in the area, searching for the danger he felt but couldn't see.

"If he's around guns, I don't want to take him by surprise. I'm going to identify myself as soon as I walk in," Kendra said, then entered the barn. "U.S. Marshal—" she called, but suddenly a hand snaked out from behind a stack of hay bales and yanked her back.

"Don't like trespassers," the burly man growled, pinning her against him in a chokehold.

Kendra stomped hard on his instep, then slammed her elbow deep into his gut. He bent over, his hold easing slightly, and she twisted free.

In the blink of an eye, Paul hurled himself at the man, tackling him to the ground.

"U.S. Marshal," Kendra snapped, moving in, weapon in hand. "Stop." The two men were still struggling, so she couldn't get a clear line of sight.

The man punched Paul in the chest, trying to break free, but Paul grabbed his arm, twisting it painfully, and rolled him onto his stomach.

The man groaned, then finally stopped resisting. "Okay, you win," he mumbled.

Paul released him, then rose to his feet and stepped back, clearing the way for Kendra.

"Don't move," Kendra said, coming up, her pistol aimed at the man's spine.

"Relax, little lady," he said, raising his head off the ground a few inches, trying to see her.

"Deputy Marshal," she corrected. "You can stow the 'little lady' routine. Now roll over and sit up. Keep your hands away from your body."

"Yes, ma'am. I had no idea you were law enforcement. We've had home invasions and break-ins around here lately, so I was just defending my place, like any man would. You didn't identify yourself until now."

"I did, right before you began to choke me," Kendra said. "Bad move. Instead of asking you a few questions and moving on, I'm placing you under arrest. Looks like you're going to be doing your talking at the closest police station."

Paul stepped away and called the local sheriff's department while Kendra kept her gun trained on the man. "You're Gil Davies, I take it?"

"That's me, so now that we've been properly introduced, you gonna tell me what you want?"

"Some information," Kendra said.

He smiled slowly. "Forget what happened here, and you might convince me to cooperate. If you take me in, forget about it."

Kendra looked him in the eye, trying to read him, but before she could answer, Paul came up and touched her on the shoulder.

"He's got a stash of black market gun parts in a box over there that can turn assault rifles into fully automatic weapons," he said.

"Looks like we'll be finishing this off at the station," Kendra said. "If you want to trim off a little prison time, Gil, start talking."

"The parts your partner saw were purchased outside a gun show in Durango. If you look in the box, you'll see the ID badge that proves I was there."

"To be in possession of those gun parts requires a boatload of specialized ATF permits. Care to show me the paperwork?"

He shrugged. "I bought them from a guy selling stuff out of his trunk in the parking lot. Just one good ole boy to another."

"Enjoy prison," Kendra said.

"So you came here just to check out gun parts?" He shook his head. "That's not what you really want to know, is it?" He smiled slowly. "Your choice. Take me in, and that's the last thing you're going to hear from me."

"Then that's the way it is. You're under arrest," Kendra said. "Turn around, and place your hands behind your back. I'm going to cuff you."

"Hey, come on. You know this'll never hold up in court. Where's your search warrant?"

Kendra smiled. "Didn't need one. You gave us permission to look in the box, remember? He just took you up on that offer."

Davis responded with a one-word curse.

It didn't take long for a deputy to show up, and Kendra remanded Davies over to the uniformed officer. "He's under federal jurisdiction, so you need to notify the marshals service. Our department will be responsible for the expense of housing the prisoner. And expect a visit from ATF on those gun parts."

Kendra made a call to that agency and reported the situation. By that time, close to noon, two more deputies had arrived on the scene, along with a search warrant based on information Kendra had forwarded.

As one deputy took Gil Davies away, others began to tape off the area in preparation for the Bureau of Alcohol, Tobacco and Firearms agent now en route from Durango, Colorado.

While the deputies worked to preserve the scene, Paul and Kendra searched the barn for any more surprises. After several minutes they met outside the barn.

"There's nothing else here for us," Paul said. "You might want to leave word for the ATF agent to contact you if there's anything in the main house that connects to Miller."

"Good idea," Kendra said. "After that, there's another lead I want to follow up."

"What's on your mind?"

She took a deep breath. "Gun shows usually have security monitors for the safety of their vendors. We need to figure out who handled that, then take a look at what they recorded from that Durango event."

"Security is Daniel's business, and if he didn't handle it, he probably knows who did. Let me give him a call."

Paul moved away as Kendra spoke to the remaining deputies about the arrival of the ATF agent. A few minutes later, she joined Paul again.

"I've got the information we need," he said. "Daniel subcontracted the job to a guy named Mickey Carson. He lives in Cortez. We passed through there on the way here, so it won't take us long to drive back. Do you want to leave now?"

"Yeah. Let's go pay him a visit. If his video of the event includes any outside surveillance, I'm going to ask to look at the footage. I'd like to try and ID the guy selling black market gun parts. It's possible he may have done business with Miller, or he might be able to point us to someone who has. Miller gets his gear under the radar, so you can bet he's got contacts all over the country."

"We're getting close to finding answers," he said as they set out. "I can feel it in my gut."

"Yeah, but in my experience, that's when things can start going wrong," she said.

"Is that what happened when you were trying to track down John Lester, the gunrunner?"

She nodded. "Lester's a slippery son-of-a-gun who's always one step ahead of whoever's after him. The other dealers want him dead because he controls a very big share of the illegal weapons market. The problem is he's got too many allies and informants," she said. "Once I capture Miller, I'll try to get reassigned to that case. I want to bring Lester down next."

He smiled. "You've got a lot of courage, Kendra, and you hate backing off. That's what I like about you."

"Yeah, I'm a fighter." Yet even as she spoke, she knew that was only partly true. In her heart she longed to surrender, to be swept away by the fires she'd found in Paul's arms.

As she glanced at Paul and saw his steady hands on the wheel, she bit back a sigh. Paul was a man trapped in the past, and he'd only break her heart. She had to keep her emotions locked safely away.

A LONG SILENCE had stretched out between them, and Paul didn't interrupt the quiet. He needed time to think. For the first time since he'd left the marshals service he thought he had a chance to find closure—to put away the man who'd killed Judy. Kendra was relentless, just the kind of partner he needed to close the case that continued to haunt his dreams.

"You said you know Mickey Carson. Any chance he's involved?" Kendra asked at last.

"I don't think so, but it'll be better if we don't assume anything."

"Yeah, better safe than sorry," she said. "The stakes are too high."

More than she even realized. Trying not to look at her, Paul kept his eyes on the road ahead. He liked being with Kendra way too much for his own good. Beneath her toughness lay a core of gentleness that drew him to her.

Many women had passed through his life over the years. Some had tried to mother him, others had offered him love, and sex, too. But his instinctive distrust of women had always kept things from going too far.

Kendra had offered him nothing more than a temporary working arrangement. She wasn't interested in a relationship, not even a physical one, though it was clear the sparks were there. Yet his feelings for her had continued to grow.

Although he could have tried to work on her emotions and persuade her to give in to the attraction between them, the final outcome would still be the same. Kendra would eventually leave and go her own way. The only thing he could do was walk on. He'd forget her…eventually.

"The video…" she said, cutting into his thoughts. "Are you sure you're ready to deal with whatever we see?"

"I don't follow. Why wouldn't I be?"

"It's possible that someone in this community, someone you know and maybe trust, is one of Miller's suppliers."

As he glanced over at her, he suddenly realized what she meant. "Wait—do you think Preston's been feeding us false information? That he's dirty? No way. He lives and breathes the job. He sees police work in Navajo terms—as restoring the balance between good and evil."

"All right, then."

"Are you really ready to let go of that idea?" he asked, watching her reaction.

She nodded. "I never thought Preston was involved, I just wanted to know where *you* stood, and that I could count on you no matter what turned up."

"You have your answer."

They arrived at Mickey Carson's upscale home outside of Cortez a while later and drove up the long, paved driveway to the front door.

Kendra, out of habit, stood to one side of the massive double doors as she rang the bell, and Paul did the same.

Moments later the door on their right opened. A tall, light-haired man around forty, wearing expensive wool slacks and a V-neck cashmere sweater, greeted them with a pleasant smile.

"Paul, it's good to see you again. Daniel called a while ago, and I've got a flash drive ready with what you need. Sorry I can't stick around. I'm meeting a new client at two o'clock."

"No prob. I've got my laptop in the truck. I'll make sure it loads, then we're gone," Paul said.

"Okay. Here's the flash drive. Let's do this."

Mickey followed them to the pickup, and on the way Paul noticed three vehicles parked under a big carport. There was a white sedan, a gray SUV, and an older model black pickup. As he glanced at Kendra, he noted that she'd also been checking out Mickey's transportation.

"Hang on while I boot it up," Paul said, bringing out his laptop. Moments later, the data files were being transferred to the laptop hard drive.

"You can manipulate the images to accentuate whatever you want," Mickey said. "You have a little over eight hours of feed there, but the files are still manageable because we used time lapse photography. Images are taken one per second, not continuously."

"Thanks, Mickey," Paul said. "Appreciate it."

"You bet."

As Mickey walked back to his house, Kendra went around to the driver's side. "Let me take the wheel, Paul. I'll drive while you deal with the laptop. It's set up for you anyway."

"Sure." He went to the passenger side, carrying his laptop. "Treat Cassie gently, okay?" he said, climbing into the cab.

"Who?" she asked, then smiled. "You gave your truck a name?"

"Yeah. Cassie's as tough as they come, but she still deserves a gentle hand," he said and winked.

As Kendra reached down to turn on the ignition, he saw the tiny smile that tugged at the corners of her mouth.

THE GRAVEL ROAD leading back to the main highway was well maintained, but a giant rooster tail of dust still trailed in a thick cloud behind them. "The drought has really taken its toll this year, even up here in southern Colorado." Paul said, rolling up his window.

Kendra slowed down to thirty miles per hour as she saw an approaching SUV traveling down the center of the road.

Paul, engrossed in the screen, said nothing.

"Move over, dummy," she muttered, honking the horn.

Paul looked up and saw the vehicle. "He's probably used to being the only driver on this road." The large, older model, green Ford SUV was closing the gap at a rapid clip.

Kendra leaned on the horn again, then inched closer to the shoulder of the road. The empty irrigation canal on her right was less than ten feet away now.

Blaring her horn, Kendra touched the brakes and eased over to the side even more. "Maybe the guy had a seizure or something."

"Or he's drunk," Paul said.

Kendra swerved across to the left, but the SUV did the same. Seconds from impact, she cut back to the right. "Hang on!"

Her heart thumping in her chest, Kendra slammed on the brakes. As the truck skidded alongside the canal, she felt the right front tire drop off. "We're going in!" she yelled, swerving into the ditch and praying they wouldn't roll over.

The pickup dropped into the ditch upright, metal screeching as the sides of the truck ricocheted back and forth off opposing banks. With one final bounce off the bank, they hit sand, slamming their heads on the roof as the truck came to an abrupt stop. A vast dirt cloud enveloped them.

Paul looked over at her immediately. "You okay?"

Kendra still had a death grip on the steering wheel. "I'm in one piece. Now I need to find a way to stop shaking."

Paul lifted the door handle and pushed, but the door only opened an inch before hitting the steep inside wall of the canal. The top of the earthen wall was at least a foot above the cab. "No clearance over here, not even through the window. How about your side?"

Kendra released the wheel and tried her door, but it wouldn't budge. "Nothing. We're jammed, and the window is right up against the bank."

Paul turned slowly, sniffing the air. "Do you smell that?"

"Gasoline. We must have ripped open the fuel line or the gas tank." She took a whiff. "I think it's coming from behind the seat, not the engine compartment. Is that better or worse?"

"I have no idea, but we better find a way out of here." Paul turned in his seat and checked the rear cab window. Through the glass he saw a man wearing a hoodie and sunglasses standing at the top of the embankment. "We've got an audience."

"Maybe it's the jerk who ran us off the road. What's he up to?" Kendra said.

Paul saw the man pull something from his pocket. Acting on instinct, he yanked Kendra down. A heartbeat later the windshield shattered, and they heard two loud pops in rapid succession, followed by a third.

"Stay down!" Paul yelled, covering her with his body.

As two more bullets struck inches from them, they heard a whooshing sound, followed by a boom that shook the truck. A blast of heat and flame erupted from the engine compartment.

Raising his head slightly, Paul saw the hood had blown open. Acrid smoke was billowing up around the front end of the truck, and vile fumes began seeping into the cab through the vents.

"We've got to get out of here right now." Gun in hand, Paul risked a look through the rear cab window, searching for the shooter, but thick black smoke obscured his view. As it was, he could barely make out the pickup bed, which was just on the other side of the glass.

"Our only chance is to break this window and squeeze through onto the bed of the truck—right into his field of view," he said, coughing hard as the air became increasingly thick.

"Go for it," she said.

"Hold my weapon," he said, handing her his pistol. He twisted around in his seat, placed his back against the passenger's side dash, and kicked the rear cab window with his boot heel. The glass cracked but held. He kicked it again, even harder than before. This time the entire window gave way, rubber seals and all, and fell into the bed of the pickup with a thump.

He took a quick look, but the guy had disappeared. "I'm going first," Paul said. "If he's still out there, I'll keep him pinned down. Hand me my weapon."

"No. I'll go first. I'm the one with the badge."

"I can get through the opening faster. You've got too many curves."

Before she could answer, he took the pistol from her hand, then angled his body up and through the narrow opening, leading with his weapon. A few seconds later, he landed on the bed of the truck with a thud.

"Still can't see him. I think he's gone," Paul yelled back, reaching for her hand. "I'll pull you through, but watch the edges. The metal is sharp."

"I'm gonna leave body parts behind for sure," she muttered, trying to protect her breasts with a forearm as she wriggled through the opening. The second half of her posed another problem. "You're built straight up and down, but I've got hips. It's just not fair."

"You're doing great," he said, standing on the flatbed of the truck and lifting her up and out.

Something in her pants pocket suddenly caught, but with a painful twist to her left, she managed to slip through.

"Thanks," she said, then took her first good look at Paul. "Your arm's covered in blood," she said, her voice rising.

He glanced down at the long tear on his sleeve, and the scrape beneath. "Aw, hell, this is just a scratch."

Paul pulled her into his arms and held her for one precious moment. Then something up front popped, and the truck shook again.

"Time to bail." Paul took her hand, they ran to the tailgate, and together they jumped down into the sandy bottom of the dry irrigation canal.

"Keep running!" he said, tugging at her hand.

They were barely fifty feet away when a thunderous explosion rocked the air. The nearly simultaneous blast of hot air threw them facedown to the ground.

Paul covered her with his body as burning truck parts rained down all around them. Seconds stretched out, and each heartbeat became an eternity. Finally, all they could hear was the roar and crackle of the fire behind them.

Paul raised his head and looked back at what was left of his truck. "Goodbye, Cassie."

"We're lucky to be alive, and your first words are 'goodbye, Cassie'?" She shook her head and pushed him off of her. "Men!"

Paul laughed and gave her a hand up. "Our luck held and we're okay," he said, reaching to wipe away a trickle of blood that was running down his forehead. "That makes this a good day."

Kendra checked her weapon, making sure the barrel and action weren't clogged with dirt, then removed her holster from her belt and emptied out the sand. Finished, she looked him over and smiled. "I look like something a cat dug up, but even dirt and blood looks good on you. How do you do that?"

He laughed. This was the side of Kendra he was sure most people never saw. The girly-girl who wanted to look good and cared about things like that even now, after crashing, dodging bullets, and almost getting fried. "You look pretty good to me, woman," he growled playfully, pulling her closer and taking her lips in a deep, satisfying kiss.

This time she didn't pull away, and heat blasted through him. As she drew back to take a breath, he saw her moist lips part. He took her mouth again, devouring her slowly.

She whimpered softly, then nuzzled the hollow of his neck. "No more. We can't."

"Death came calling for us today, but we're still here. Celebrate life with me. No more wasted moments."

He took her mouth again, not giving her a chance to protest. The way she melted against him nearly drove him over the edge.

"No," she managed with a broken sigh and moved away. "We can't wait around here in the open. We have to find some place safe."

"The guy who did this probably thinks we're dead, but you're right. We need to leave in case he decides to come back and make sure," he said.

"Any suggestions? Your friend Mickey's not at home, so hiking back there is out."

"How about Two Springs Ranch? It's in the area and belongs to my brother Gene," Paul said. "He'll come get us and provide a safe place for as long as we need. I trust him—with my life and yours."

Chapter Fifteen

An hour later Kendra was riding in the back seat of Gene's four-wheel drive SUV. The Colorado state patrol officer had assured her that they'd sealed off the crime scene and that an ATL, attempt to locate, was out on the shooter and his green Ford SUV. The problem was that in this ranching community that was a common make of vehicle, and tracking down the right one would take time.

Gene soon braked to a stop and went to open the gate leading to Two Springs Ranch. He was still saying goodbye to someone on his cell phone when he returned. "Just checking. My wife keeps the bunkhouse ready for guests."

"So Kendra and I are going to rough it?" Paul said, grinning.

"Not at all. You haven't seen the changes we've made since you were here last," Gene said, then looked at Kendra and explained. "The bunkhouse was initially supposed to be the rancher equivalent of a man cave, but Lori had different plans." He glanced back at his brother. "So, should I get Doc Riley to drive over and take a look at you two?"

"Let me guess. He's your vet?" Paul asked.

Gene laughed. "No, he's an M.D. He had a big city practice, retired, then decided he didn't want to sit around doing nothing all day long. He bought the ranch north of here next to Deer Trail Creek and donates time to a clinic in Dolores. He even makes house calls a couple of days a week."

"I don't need a doc," Paul said, then glanced at Kendra. "I think you should have one look you over, though."

"No thanks. I'm scraped up and bruised, but nothing worse than a bad day at the gym," she said.

Paul didn't argue. She was back to being Deputy Marshal Armstrong now, and Kendra would call anything short of gushing blood a scrape. He smiled. She was some kind of woman—his kind of woman.

The realization slammed into him. He was falling in love with Kendra—hard. He stared at her for a moment longer than he should have.

"You okay?" she asked. "You look...confused."

"Nah, I'm just sorting things out." The truth of it was he had no business falling in love with anyone. Until Judy's killer was behind bars, his life wasn't his own. He owed a debt to the past—one that needed to be repaid.

"I've got a bottle of twelve-year-old single malt scotch in the cabinet for you," Gene said, glancing at Paul.

"Still the best painkiller I know," he replied.

As Gene parked in front of the bunkhouse, Paul looked over at Kendra and saw the smile on her face.

"You into country living?" Paul asked her.

"I wouldn't go that far, but this place is just so welcoming," she said. "I love the white painted wood, bright yellow chairs, and just look at that porch swing for two."

"That's mostly Lori's doing," Gene said proudly. "Before, there was only a log bench and hitching post. Come on, let me show you the inside."

Gene opened the door and invited them in with a wave of his hand. "There's not much in the mini fridge here, so come over to the main house when you're ready to eat."

"Where's Lori?" Paul asked glancing around. "Cooking up a storm?"

"Nah. She's shopping in Cortez, but she'll be back by eight. She left dinner for me, but, as usual, she made enough to feed an army, so you're invited to dig in. There's a batch of fresh homemade chocolate chip cookies, too."

"Bro, she's got you eating right out of her hand," Paul teased.

"Don't knock it till you've tried it," he said, then nodded to Kendra. "There's a shower in the small bathroom at the end of this hall, but you'll only get cold water there. The big bathroom with the claw-footed bathtub has cold and hot running water—and the tub fits two."

Kendra nearly choked. "I bathe alone."

Gene looked at Paul with raised eyebrows and shrugged.

"One more thing before you go," Paul said, playfully shoving Gene back toward the door. "Where do you keep the first aid kit?"

"Bathroom cabinet. You'll find plenty of supplies there. Lori insisted on it after Preston and Daniel put on the gloves and turned the corral into a boxing ring one evening. They'd decided to work out their frustrations after the fifty dollar pay-per-view match they'd been watching lasted less than two minutes."

"Who won, Preston or Daniel?" Kendra asked.

"Neither. Lori turned the hose on them as soon as Preston got a bloody lip," Gene said, laughing.

"Speaking of bloody," Paul said, glancing down at his clothing. "Can I borrow a change of clothing?"

"Daniel keeps a few shirts and pants in the first bedroom. You and Dan wear the same size, right?" He glanced at Kendra. "You're about the same size as Daniel's wife, Holly. She keeps some jeans and sweaters in there, too. Feel free to borrow whatever you need. They won't mind. I think there's some makeup stuff in there, too, but I don't know jack about that."

Paul walked outside with Gene. "Thanks for coming to pick us up," he said.

"No prob. Clean up and relax with the lady. I'll stay away."

"No need, nothing's going to happen."

Gene shook his head. "Maybe something *should*. I saw the way you look at her." Not giving him a chance to answer, Gene walked away.

Paul expelled his breath in a hiss. Were his feelings for Kendra that obvious? He strode back inside and found Kendra running her hand along the tongue and groove, knotty pine walls.

"This is so beautiful," she said, standing at the doorway to one of the rooms. "It's real wood, and the grain's perfect."

"It used to be one big room with bunk beds and a potbelly stove in the middle. Lori has been pressuring Gene to make the place better-suited to adults. I can see she won that battle."

"She's done a great job. Look at this vanity table. I bet she made the organza skirt around it. It's so pretty."

"In a bunkhouse…"

"It's extra special precisely because it's *in* a bunkhouse. It welcomes women, not just men."

"I guess," he replied.

She glanced back at him. "What's wrong?"

"Just sore and crabby," he said, but as he tried to shrug, he winced.

"Is it your shoulder again?"

"Nah, I scraped my back when I crawled out of the pickup window," he said. "I recall I was in a hurry at the time."

"Take off your shirt and let me take a look. You might need that doctor after all."

"It's not that bad," he said, but he shrugged out of his shirt anyway and set his fetish aside.

"Turn around," she said softly.

As her fingertips brushed his skin, he suppressed a shudder—and not from the pain.

"You're more scraped up than me, so you get to clean up first. Once you're out of the bathtub, I'll put some antiseptic on those cuts."

"Then I'll do the same for you."

"My scrapes have sealed up. I'm fine," she said.

He pointed to her shoulder. "Not really. You're still bleeding a bit. See where your sweater's sticking to the cut? You don't want to get any of that soot and grime in there. Better take it off so we can have a look."

He saw the flash of excitement that lit her eyes, and that look pleased him far more than it should have.

"Never mind. I'll grab some clothes and go take a bath," she said, then looked at her hands and winced. "Ugh. On second thought, I need to wash my hands first. Pretty disgusting, huh?"

"I have to disagree." He pulled her into his arms and kissed her gently. "You're beautiful," he murmured, drawing back and enjoying the hazy look in her eyes as she gazed back at him.

"Why can't I stop wanting you?" she whispered, but this time she didn't pull away. "I know what I have to do...."

"You can't be strong all the time. No one can," he said, kissing her again.

"Not even you?"

"Particularly me," he said. "I need...you."

He kissed her shoulder, then her neck, loving the way she melted into him. "Even the strong need love, sweetheart, more than we'll ever admit."

She drew in a breath as he gently lifted off her sweater, unclasped her bra and kissed her breasts. "My knees are about to buckle. I'm not that strong."

"You need me as much as I need you. Stop thinking. Just feel."

He grasped her buttocks and pressed her into him. He was hard and ready, but he'd hold back. He'd burn these moments into her memory forever.

"Before you came into my life, I was cold and empty inside. You've given my heart a reason for beating again." He took her soft breast into his mouth.

Gasping, she wrapped her arms around him. "I want...." Her words trailed off as he nipped at the taut peak gently.

"Tell me," he demanded in a rough whisper.

"I want to surrender...then feel you go wild inside me."

The words lit a fire in his blood. He lifted her into his arms and carried her to the bed.

"Set me down," she said quickly. "You'll hurt your shoulder...."

"What shoulder?" All he could feel now was the fire—pure, sweet, and furnace-hot.

He eased her onto the soft mattress, brushing away what remained of her clothing and kissing her everywhere. He kept his touch gentle, wanting to bring her to the edge many times before they were through. He knew what would give her pleasure.

"This was meant to happen," he murmured, opening her to his touch.

She gasped with pleasure and arched upwards toward him. "No, not yet," she managed, struggling to hold back. "You've still got your jeans on. Let me see you."

He stood beside the bed, unbuckled his belt, and stripped. "Like what you see?" he growled, standing there, letting her gaze sear over him.

"You're so beautiful," she managed in a choked whisper.

"Nobody's ever called me that."

She opened her arms and reached out to him. "Look at me when you slip inside my body. I love the way your eyes darken when you want me."

Seeing her wanting and needing him made him crazy. Holding her gaze, he settled over her. "How could I not look at you now?"

She wasn't sure how long she slept, but when she awoke she found herself encircled in his powerful arms. His chest moved with each breath as she lay with her head on his left shoulder.

"You're awake," he said.

"How did you know? Your eyes were closed."

"Yes, but I wasn't asleep. I was enjoying the warmth of your body against mine."

She nestled deeper into his arms and sighed contentedly. "We can't lie here forever. It's seven o'clock in the evening."

"My brother won't bother us."

She laughed softly. "Have him trained, do you?" she said, sitting up.

"He knows I've got feelings for you," he said.

"Do you?" she asked softly.

He started to reach for his jeans, then stopped and turned his head to look at her. "I thought I was pretty clear about that." He gestured back to the bed. "Complaints?"

She shook her head and smiled. "You were gentle when you needed to be and rough and wonderful at other times," she said, getting up.

Only one thing had kept it from being perfect. He'd never really told her how he felt about her.

Almost as if Paul had read her unspoken thought, he pulled her against him. "I care about you, Kendra, and that's not something I say lightly. In fact, I've never said that to anyone before."

The revelation didn't surprise her. She looked up at him, sensing he had more to say.

"These days, people use the word 'love' too easily. To me, love means the willingness to make the other person a part of your life, but that's not a place you can be right now. My life will never be my own until my past is settled."

She nodded. That kind of loyalty was rare and beautiful. "No promises were made and none need to be kept," she said.

He stood tall, confident in his nakedness. "Regrets?"

"None," she said.

He took a step closer to her, his body growing hard again. But hearing a car pulling up in the gravel, he stopped.

Paul went to the window and, standing to one side, looked out. "Two of my brothers are here," he said.

"I'll bathe fast, then you can go clean up."

"No hurry. I'll use the shower. The cold water will do me good."

Chapter Sixteen

Kendra bathed, then dressed quickly. Stopping to look at herself in the mirror, she studied her reflection. The pale peach turtleneck sweater and snug jeans accentuated her feminine curves.

"You look nice," he said, standing in the doorway.

"These clothes will have to do, but they don't really suit me," she said.

"They may not suit Deputy U.S. Marshal Armstrong, but they do suit the you I've come to know."

Kendra avoided looking at him. It was time to get down to business. To emphasize it to herself, she clipped her badge onto her belt. "Sexy and feminine clash big-time with my weapon and holster," she said with a quick half smile. "There's a jacket in there, and I think I'm going to put it over this sweater."

He nodded, then walked down the hall.

A few moments later, she met him in the living room.

"You look the part, Deputy Marshal, and you'll fit right in with law enforcement here in the Four Corners," he said.

"Good." She rolled up the cuffs another notch. "This jacket will hide my holster and badge—unless I choose to have them show."

Minutes later they walked over to the main house. As they went through the unlocked kitchen door, Paul heard the crackle of the fireplace and loud, familiar voices arguing in the next room.

"They're both targets," Preston was saying. "The evidence speaks for itself."

"Don't kid yourself. Without a clear motive, we're still just guessing," Daniel answered.

"They've been ducking bullets for days now. What else do you need?" Gene said.

"Guys," Paul said, walking into the room.

"Hey, good to see you're both okay. I figured I'd give you about another ten minutes, then call the paramedics," Gene said with a quick grin.

"Yeah, yeah," Paul growled then looked at Preston. "What brought you here? Did you turn up something?"

He shook his head. "I read the bulletin and knew you'd be here. The state patrol is still looking over the crime scene, so why don't you tell me how it all went down?"

"The gunman was above us on the bank, firing blind into the cab," Paul said. "There was a lot of smoke, and the side windows were below ground level."

"Which side of the cab took the bulk of the hits—driver's or passenger's?" Preston asked, zeroing in on the question foremost in their minds. "Do you know?"

"The driver's side took the first few hits. The rounds came through the lower roof and rear of the cab," Kendra said. "The steering wheel hub took a hit, and there were at least two more through the driver's side backrest. The way I see it, they were grouped to cover that half of the interior."

"Did the shooter know who was driving?" Daniel asked.

"Yeah, he knew. We passed by so close there was no way for him to miss that," Kendra said. "Paul pulled me down across the cab, and the bullets passed just over my legs. If I'd stayed behind the wheel I'd be dead."

"I still don't get it. What were you doing on that road in the first place?" Preston asked.

"We'd just picked up a flash drive from Mickey," Paul said, telling him about the gun show surveillance feed.

"So, once again, though it looks like we're dealing with a marksman, he still missed his target?" Daniel said.

"This time it wasn't for lack of trying," Paul said. "Combine that with the fact that he ran us off the road, and that alone could have easily killed us, and you're looking at what was clearly a hit."

"But why are you being targeted? What's the motive here?" Preston said.

"You tell me. I suspect an informant in the marshals service, but as I said, I have no proof," Kendra said.

"From where I sit, it looks like the informant is someone close to both of you," Daniel said, looking at Kendra, then Paul.

"It's no one I associate with," Paul said. "I haven't had any special contact with the marshals service in eight or nine months."

"I'm sure you have your own source there, a friend who has kept you current on the status of the investigation?" Kendra said, taking a guess. "Who is it?"

He shook his head. "Couldn't be him. He's completely loyal to the marshals service."

"I'm with Kendra on this. We should still look into it," Preston said. "I could check him out—discreetly, of course."

"No, you don't get it," Paul said. "He retired two months ago. My guy's out of the loop, and what's been happening to us is recent."

"Okay, but keep thinking about it," Preston said. "Who could it be?"

Paul said nothing for several long moments, standing in front of the fireplace, staring at the flames.

Minutes stretched out. Kendra started to speak, but Preston shook his head.

She waited.

Paul finally turned to face them. "The hit on the judge happened ten months ago. No one's come after me since then. So why now? What's changed?"

"I asked myself that just the other day. I figured once I found the answer, I could use it to draw Miller out," Kendra said. "Nothing's come to light, so now I don't know. Do you think that maybe it's taken them this long to get to you because they figured you weren't going anywhere?"

"Not likely. That kind of business doesn't get put on hold," Paul said. "I've got another idea we need to consider. What if you were right, Kendra, and *you* were the primary target all along? The hit on me could have been arranged so that your supervisor would be pressured to send you here—away from where you might have done serious damage. Having you killed while hunting down Miller could have also permanently obscured the real motive for the hit."

Kendra stared at him for a moment, his words sinking in. "If you're right, that's a brilliant plan."

"So, now what?" Daniel asked.

"We go back to one of the primary questions," Preston said. "Someone has been feeding the gunman information on your whereabouts. Let's narrow it down. Who knows where you are?" he asked Kendra.

"My supervisor, Evan Thomas, his office assistant, his boss and anyone else in the chain of command who has access to the reports," Kendra said.

Her cell phone, inside the pocket of her shirt, began to ring. She glanced at the caller ID. "It's Evan, do you believe it? I have to take this. By now, he's seen the Colorado patrol's report."

"Don't give out your current location if you can help it," Preston warned.

Kendra nodded and stepped into the kitchen. "Armstrong," she said, answering the call.

"I just heard about the incident that went down earlier

today, but there was no medical report. You okay?" Thomas asked.

"I'm fine, Evan," she said. "I was tracking down a lead to Miller when I got run off the road and into an empty irrigation canal. The suspect then shot the vehicle full of holes. He missed, and we got out just after the truck caught on fire."

"Were you able to ID your assailant?"

"No. It could have been Miller, but conditions prevented us from getting a good look at the suspect."

"I need results, Armstrong, and you're getting nowhere," he snapped. "I've got people breathing down my neck here, and I'm tired of making excuses. Unless you can bring Miller in, or at least track his location, I'm going to have to come down there myself."

Having her supervisor question her abilities for the second time in days hit her hard. "I'll find Miller."

"Don't let me down, Kendra. You've got a week," he said.

Hearing nothing but dead air, she realized Thomas had ended the call. She stared at the phone in her hand, her emotions flipping back and forth between exasperation and anger.

"What's wrong?" Paul said, coming up to her.

"Nothing."

"Yeah, right. Your eyes are flashing hot and cold, and you've got a death grip on that phone."

"My boss is a tool. Now my job—my reputation—is on the line." She recounted her conversation with Evan. "I've never failed to get results, not once. Sure, sometimes it took everything I had, but I always came through. Now, twice in a row, I've come up short." She gripped the countertop, lost in thought. "What irks me most is that by telling me he'll take over, he's saying he can do something I can't."

"Like I've mentioned before, I know Thomas. He was trying to motivate you, not rattle you. He'll play with your head if he thinks it'll make you better at your job." Paul said. "Evan was my supervisor, too, for a while. When my partner went down, he was right on the scene. He helped me get a handle on things. He's good at what he does."

Kendra exhaled slowly and glanced around. "He's still a tool. Any chocolate around here?"

Gene came in just then and laughed. "Sounds like you and my wife have something in common, Kendra, but I'm afraid I finished the last of the chocolate peanut butter cups. Lori was going grocery shopping today. I'm guessing she'll be getting a fresh supply."

"Then I'm going for a walk," she said. "Don't worry, I won't go far, and I'll keep my weapon handy."

"Even so, let me take a look around first," Gene said.

"I'll go with you," Daniel said, coming up behind him.

TWENTY MINUTES LATER, Kendra stood with Paul by the corral, illuminated by an overhead lamp on a post, and watched the trio of horses browsing through scattered alfalfa leaves on the ground.

"It's so incredibly peaceful here," she said, taking a breath of fresh air.

"Yeah, it is. There was a time in my life when I couldn't understand why Gene or anyone else would want to live all the way out here, running a ranch so far from the city," Paul said. "Standing here right now, I've got to say it doesn't seem like such a bad idea."

She turned around and leaned against the welded pipe fence railing. "When I first joined the marshals service I was in love with the idea of an exciting career, something far from the ordinary."

"And now?" he asked.

"I still love my work, but I've also discovered I need more than the job to be happy. Someday I'd like a family of my own." She looked at Paul and gave him a wry smile. "Don't panic. I'm not angling for a proposal just because we made love."

"Would that be so bad?"

"Bad? No," she managed, apparently surprised at his response.

"You know what our problem is?" she said, smiling. "Some people need fresh air, but our brains need car exhaust fumes to function right."

"Maybe so," Paul said, laughing. He placed a boot on the lower rail and leaned over, resting. As he did, one of the horses came up to him and nickered softly.

He glanced up, expecting to see Bud, or maybe Clyde, Lori's favorite horse. To his surprise, it was Grit.

"What a beautiful pinto! That jet-black head and perfect white blaze down his nose is really eye-catching," Kendra said.

Paul stared at the animal, then patted his neck cautiously, half expecting Grit to spin and try to kick him, or make a bite threat. Maybe in the dim light the horse had mistaken him for someone else. Yet even as the thought formed, he realized how unlikely that was. Horses had a good sense of sight and smell.

Gene, who'd been coming toward them, stopped and stared.

"Can you believe this?" Paul said to his brother.

"You stopped forcing it, and things worked out on their own," Gene said. He glanced at Kendra, then back at Paul. "Remember *Hosteen* Silver's prediction."

Paul nodded, then looked at Kendra. "I only told you part of it. Would you like to hear all of it?" Seeing her nod, he continued. "When Dark Thunder speaks in the silence, enemies will become friends, and friends, enemies. Lynx will bring more questions, but it's Grit who'll show you the way if you become his friend. Life and death will call, but in the end, you'll choose your own path."

"We just escaped death, and Grit's here to show you the way...to life?" she asked, petting the horse.

Paul spoke softly, noticing how the horse nuzzled her. "I think *Hosteen* Silver was telling me to look to the future and not dwell on the past. If I continue fighting to find justice for my partner's murder, more blood may be spilled, but I've got no other choice. A killer is out there, one who won't stop until he's brought down."

"Then you've made your decision," Gene said.

"I've also got a plan," Paul said. "Let's go back inside. Kendra and I will need Preston's help."

Chapter Seventeen

Paul laid out the details of his plan, then looked at the others gathered around the room. "There are no guarantees, but if we follow through with this we'll find out once and for all if Kendra's the gunman's primary target. Once we know that, our other questions will be answered, too."

"I don't like this at all, but I don't see a way around it either," Preston said, then continued. "If we're going to do this, you should use one of our department's safe houses in Hartley. There are three, but the one I have in mind is unoccupied right now, and the houses on both sides of it are empty, too. That entire neighborhood has been hit with one foreclosure after another."

"You're asking me to lie to my supervisor, Paul," Kendra said slowly. "That kind of thing has serious consequences, and Evan's bound to find out eventually."

"That's true," Paul said, "but can you think of anything else we can do at this point?"

She said nothing for several long moments, and no one interrupted the silence even as the minutes ticked by. "No, unfortunately, I can't," she said at last.

"Then it's a go?" Preston asked.

"Yes," Paul said, "but we need to make sure that the only people in the loop are ones we trust one hundred percent. That means the list will be short—Preston, Daniel, Gene, Kendra and me. Kendra and I will be at the safe house while the rest of you will be close by, providing backup."

"One second," Preston said. "My career is on the line and this is my turf, so *I'm* calling the shots. Agreed?"

As the others nodded, Preston continued. "Kendra, time to put things in motion. Call your supervisor and tell him that you'll be staying at one of our P.D.'s safe houses and you're waiting for directions. You can say that you've picked a place that's off the radar—not connected to any part of your fugitive retrieval assignment—since Miller's shown he can find you easily. If he asks about Paul, tell him that he's working out other arrangements, but you haven't been briefed yet."

"I'll do it right now," she said.

Kendra picked up her cell phone and dialed Evan Thomas. It was nine at night now, so she had to call his cell. He answered on the fourth ring, and she stuck to the script.

"File a report through channels," he snapped. "The next thing I want to hear from you is that you've found Miller."

She gritted her teeth and politely finished the call. "Let's get going," she said, reaching for her jacket. "Evan isn't the only one running out of patience. If Miller's out there, his days as a free man are coming to a close."

ON THE WAY back to Hartley, Paul was quiet. They'd borrowed Gene's new truck for the time being, and as he drove, he constantly checked in the rearview mirror.

"Your brothers are always there for you. That must be a very nice feeling, to know someone always has your back."

"You have your brother and father. They're both military men who live by a strict code of conduct and honor. They'd do the same for you."

"If it came down to it, sure, but the closeness isn't there. Their lives are halfway around the world."

"Not all my brothers are living close by. As a matter of fact, two are overseas right now. Once they left home, Rick and Kyle wanted to go as far away from the Rez as possible," he said. "Now that it's out of their systems, they'll be coming home as soon as their rotation is up. Their roots are here."

"I think it's your cultural ties that really help strengthen the bond between all of you," she said.

"They do, that's true. The traditions of our people—concepts like 'walking in beauty'—shape our lives," he said. "Explaining our ways to outsiders is hard because when we try, it often comes across as stilted English—a bunch of odd-sounding phrases all strung together."

"Those who care enough to want to understand, will."

He smiled. "And if not, it's their loss. We're proud of who and what we are. That's part of *Hosteen* Silver's legacy."

"He sounds like a remarkable man," she said.

"He was. His death left a huge gap in our lives," he said. "It also took us by complete surprise."

"What happened, if you don't mind my asking?"

"He walked off into the desert one winter night without any explanation and his body was never found. That's the way of our Traditionalists when they believe death is near, but the thing is, he wasn't sick, not that we knew about anyway."

"Did he leave anything behind that might have explained why he did that?"

"There was one clue—of sorts. He left us a retelling of a Navajo creation story, one meant to show that good can be corrupted by evil, but that evil can always be defeated by those who remain strong," Paul said. "Now it's up to us to find the answer hidden there."

"He wasn't one for speaking plainly, I take it?"

"He would when necessary, but *Hosteen* Silver believed that when you grappled with a question, you often found answers to things you never even thought to ask."

"Maybe you need someone who can view it from an outsider's perspective. If you tell me the story, I'll try to help," she said.

"All right." After a moment he began to tell her the tale, his voice soft, yet oddly compelling. "Changing-Bear-Woman was a beautiful maiden who had many suitors. Coyote wanted to marry her, but she wanted no part of him. Trying to discourage him, she gave him a list of impossible challenges. Coyote agreed to all her demands but, in return, made her promise that she'd marry him if he succeeded. Eventually, Coyote found ways to fulfill all of the tasks, so she became his wife."

"That was good, right? I mean, she kept her word."

"Yes, but soon Coyote began to teach her about the power of evil. In time, she learned how to change into a bear. That's when she stopped being who she'd been, an honorable mortal woman, and became an evil monster that needed to be stopped."

"Did Coyote do that himself?"

He shook his head. "Once she became evil, Coyote didn't like her anymore, so he walked out on her. Angry and feeling betrayed, she went looking for him. During her search she ended up killing everyone who got in her way, including most of her brothers."

"But not all?"

"The youngest one escaped, but seeing the lives she'd claimed, he realized that his sister was gone forever. To restore the balance between good and evil, he knew he'd have to destroy the creature that now stood in his sister's place. He prepared himself to do what was necessary, but wanting to somehow honor who she'd once been, he allowed her to live on in other forms that continue to serve the Diné, the Navajo People. A part of her body became the first piñon nut, another yucca fruit and so on."

"So in the end, evil was conquered and served the ultimate good," she said, understanding. "That could be said to be a cautionary tale, particularly for those of us in law enforcement. We tend to see things in black and white—legal or illegal. That's our job. Maybe this was your foster father's way of saying that good needs evil and evil needs good. The battle between the two defines each side."

He considered her words. "You may have something there. That's very much in line with Navajo thinking. We believe that everything has two sides. That's how balance is achieved."

"Maybe Mister Silver knew he had an illness that couldn't be controlled. His way of restoring harmony was to greet death," she said softly.

"No. Though what you're saying sounds logical, it doesn't feel right to me," Paul said.

"Sometimes it takes a long time to find the truth. We see that in investigations all the time."

"And like it was with Grit, I can't force it."

"Exactly.

"You've given me something to think about," he said. "Thanks."

"Glad I could help."

"Before I met you, I'd never spoken about *Hosteen* Silver's letters to anyone outside my family." He took her hand and gave it a squeeze. "There've been a lot of firsts for me since you came into my life."

She sighed. "And that's bound to make facing down Miller, or whoever comes after us, harder. You realize that, don't you?"

"Maybe, but we're trained for this and we're not alone," he said.

"If Miller doesn't show up and all we end up collaring is a minor player, I'll have to come up with a plan to force Miller out into the open. I'm not going back empty-handed," she said.

"I now know what your fetish should be," he said, a slow smile tugging at the corners of his mouth. "It's practically tailor-made for you."

"What?"

"Let me surprise you."

"If I promise to act surprised later, will you tell me now?"

He laughed. "You'll know when the time is right."

THEY ARRIVED AT the safe house in Hartley an hour later. It was in a middle class neighborhood filled with single family homes whose owners had fallen on hard times since the real estate market's free fall. Several of the houses were listed for sale and appeared to be mostly foreclosures, judging from their state of disrepair.

The safe house was in the middle of a cul-de-sac. There was a high cinder block wall in the rear, bordering a warehouse protected by dogs, judging from the signs, so the only real access was from street side.

A minute later Kendra and Paul were inside the sturdy brick house. It was plain and utilitarian but well laid out and solidly constructed.

After finishing the delicious take-out Navajo tacos Preston had brought, Kendra and Paul were alert once again, weapons easily accessible, as they kept an eye on the street. Having already taken up their positions, Preston and Daniel were hidden outside. It was close to ten-thirty, so there were few cars passing by and no neighbors out walking.

As per the plan, Kendra made it a point to cross in front of the window periodically, allowing herself to be seen, but never walking slowly enough to turn herself into an easy target. Keeping the table lamp and a TV on with the sound down so they could hear anyone approaching, they still hoped to create the illusion that they were easy prey.

After two long, boring hours, Paul was at the fridge grabbing another cola for himself when the tactical radio positioned on the coffee table crackled to life. The next thing they heard was Daniel's voice.

"There's a four-door sedan coming up the street, going real slow."

"Paul, Kendra, stay out of sight," Preston said next. "I'm on the north side of the house behind cover, watching the street. It could be just a resident coming home from an evening shift, so stay cool."

Paul was already by the front window, off to the side, and behind the curtain as he watched the street with night vision binoculars. "He's slowing, like he's checking addresses," he told the others.

Paul reached down for the tenth time in the past two hours and rested his hand on the butt of his weapon. "I can't make out the driver, but I think he's male, judging from the short hair."

"He's going to stop…here," Kendra said, standing across from Paul behind the other curtained window.

"Hold your positions. Maybe it's an officer," Preston said.

The driver pulled up into the driveway and parked. As the car door opened and the dome light came on, the face of the driver became clear.

"I've got an ID. It's my boss, Evan Thomas," Kendra said quickly.

Paul came over, his binoculars lowered. "I thought you didn't give him your location."

"I didn't, at least not which one. He didn't ask, and I didn't volunteer," Kendra said. "I don't know how he tracked me."

"He must have hopped on the next available flight after you two spoke, or maybe he was already making the drive down from Denver," Paul said.

"Stand down," Preston called over the radio to the others. "He's not packing a weapon."

Thomas opened the passenger door on the driver's side and reached inside. "Give me a hand with this gear, Armstrong, will you?" he yelled. "I know you saw me pull up."

"I better help him out. Evan's the best special ops sniper in the Rockies, and he never goes anywhere without his weapon," Kendra said, moving to the door.

Kendra stepped out onto the front porch, her weapon holstered now, then walked across the remnants of the lawn toward Thomas's car. "How did you know where I was?"

"Gun!" Paul suddenly yelled from inside. "Driveway—across the street!"

Kendra dove to the grass, rolling as three shots rang out. Out of the corner of her eye, she saw Thomas flinch, then fall to the driveway, groaning.

Pistol out, she squeezed off two of the six or seven rounds that suddenly erupted from all around her, all aimed at the gun flashes coming from a hundred feet away. The shooter, barely visible before, tumbled to the ground.

"Cover me," Paul yelled to his brothers, then ran to Kendra's side. "You okay?"

Kendra was already on one knee, her weapon trained on the fallen target. "I'm fine, but Evan took a hit."

"Hold your positions! Look for a second shooter," Preston yelled, then ran out from behind the corner of the house.

Preston continued across the yard to where Supervisory Inspector Evan Thomas sat, his back against the side of the car.

"I'm fine," Thomas said. "The round went through my arm. Check out the shooter."

A porch light came on in a house farther down the street, and an elderly woman poked her head outside. "What's all that racket?"

"Go back inside, ma'am," Preston yelled out to her as he crossed the street. "I'm a police officer and there's been a shooting."

Preston reached the downed perp and, using his foot, pushed aside the Ruger carbine that lay next to him. "The shooter's alive. Call 911, Dan," he yelled to his brother, who was standing in front of the house to Kendra's left.

"Already on it," Dan said.

Kendra crouched by Evan, who was now holding a blood-soaked handkerchief against his upper arm.

"Wanna get a first aid kit? I'm losing a lot of blood here," he said, his tone a professional blend of anger and pain.

"I'll see what I can find," Kendra said.

Paul joined Preston by the gunman, who lay on the grass beside the concrete drive, his breathing shallow and labored. He'd taken multiple hits but was wearing a vest, and the rounds that had struck his torso hadn't penetrated. He was bleeding heavily, however, from two hits to his upper thigh. The man would live if he had immediate care, which was on the way.

Preston placed a handkerchief over the leg wounds, applying pressure to reduce the flow of blood. "Hold this in place if you want to live," he ordered. The wounded man complied without comment.

Paul looked at the gunman's sunburned face, concentrating on the eyes. "Miller," Paul said in a quiet voice. "About time we met up close."

The man made eye contract, but there was no discernible expression on his face.

"I'll need a positive ID," Preston said. Crouching down, he pressed the suspect's finger to his cell phone's screen, sending the image to a database thousands of miles away. "Chris Miller," Preston said a moment later. "A perfect match to his military prints."

"You're going down hard," Paul told the wounded man, who continued to stare back at him blankly. "You killed a federal marshal, which means life as you know it has come to an end."

Kendra came over and crouched next to Miller. "You're never going to see freedom again, but *if* you give us the name of the person who hired you, we might be able to cut a deal. Think about it. Maximum security prison time safely away from the cartel's hit men, versus lethal injection."

Miller said nothing.

"I know you came looking for me at the coffee shop, impersonating an officer," Paul said, but Miller still didn't react. "The evidence we've already got will bury you. Get smart and cooperate. You're a liability to your former employer now, with makes you a soon-to-be dead man. Without some form of protective custody, it's just a matter of days or weeks."

This time Miller looked away and closed his eyes.

"You're an excellent marksman, yet you failed three times trying to kill Paul, my supervisor and me," Kendra said. "The big question is, why? You gave me a chance, and now I'm giving you one in return. You need protection, and we need your testimony."

Miller opened his eyes and looked at her for the first time.

"That's all I can offer you," she said.

The sound of approaching sirens filled the air, and as the paramedics arrived, Kendra rose to her feet and waved them closer.

FORTY MINUTES LATER Kendra sat by Preston's desk at the station. Both Chris Miller and Evan Thomas were in the regional medical center, protected by local police officers and hospital security.

Preston placed Chris Miller's file in front of Kendra, but after a quick look, she realized she'd had nearly identical copies on her laptop for days. "There's nothing here I don't already know. Miller's strictly a gun for hire, a freelancer with no real ties or allegiances. With him, it's all about the money. We need the person who hired him, and that's information only he can give. Without that, we're only buying time. His employer will just send a new shooter after us."

"What I want to know is how Inspector Thomas found you. We never gave him your location," Paul said.

"Yeah, we did," Preston said. "Supervisory Inspector Thomas called my captain earlier today on another matter. Kendra's name came up, and Captain Johnson told him where she'd be. He knew I'd requested the safe house on her behalf."

Seeing Paul's expression harden, he glared back at him. "I'm part of a police department, bro, and we have protocols to follow. Without going through those channels, I wouldn't have been able to use the place."

"Okay, one mystery solved," Kendra said. "Now here's another. I'm guessing that the leak in the marshals service took Miller to Thomas, but I still don't understand why my boss suddenly became a target, too," Kendra said. "Anyone?" she asked, looking at Paul, then Preston.

Preston shrugged. "We need to gather more evidence and identify at least another player or two before motives become clear. For now, let's concentrate on the physical evidence we have," Preston said. "Miller's Chevy, which was stolen earlier today, is still at the crime scene. Officers discovered it parked one street over from the safe house. The tags were stolen, along with the car."

"So the crime scene unit is processing the car right now?" Kendra asked.

He nodded. "Here's what we've got so far." He looked down at the small notebook he pulled from his pocket. "With Miller, there was the carbine and two spare magazines loaded with nine millimeter ammunition. In the stolen vehicle we found a smart phone under the driver's seat, and a disguise kit—two wigs, a mustache with stickum on the back, and a beard with the same type of adhesive. There was also a tube of rubber cement."

"Anything yet on the carbine?" she asked.

"The serial number was run, and the weapon was traced to an estate sale in Arizona. We've got people trying to contact the seller to see if they kept a record on the buyer," Preston said, then shrugged. "Private sales…you know how that goes."

"Yeah. Usually impossible to trace. Was there a navigation unit in the vehicle?" Kendra asked.

"Yes, but Miller knew how to disable the system, which means we can't trace his travel route after the vehicle was stolen."

"I'd like to revisit the crime scene and take a look around," Kendra said. "Since I can't speak to Evan yet and Miller's still in surgery, maybe I find something that'll give us a few more answers. I came here to collar Miller, and I've done that, but now I've got to make sure he stays alive. He's a potential federal witness and the next likely target of whoever's running this operation."

"Yeah. It's clear Miller wasn't working alone. The fact that he was able to take his shot right after Thomas arrived proves it," Paul said.

"Exactly. Miller had to have known Evan's movements, down to the exact address of his destination," Kendra said. "He was already set up to take the shot by the time Thomas got there."

"Good point," Preston said. "One thing—since all this is taking place on my turf now, I want to be kept current on whatever you find."

"Consider it done," Kendra said.

"We know where he ended up, but where was Miller staying?" Paul asked Preston. "Does the department know yet?"

"He didn't have any key cards or house keys with him, but we're on that now. I'll let you know."

Paul and Kendra left the station shortly thereafter and walked directly to Gene's truck.

"My gut's telling me that the answers we're looking for are staring us right in the face," Paul said.

"Once we're able to question Miller again we'll get what we need," Kendra said.

"I'm not so sure. He's a hard case. I've seen his type before. He'd rather rot in jail for the rest of his miserable life than give us anything," Paul replied.

"He heard my offer. When he wakes up and realizes how vulnerable he is now, unarmed and immobile, I think he'll come to his senses and cooperate," Kendra said.

After ten minutes of light traffic, they arrived back at the safe house. Yellow crime scene tape cordoned off the area where Miller had gone down, and the crime scene team was spread out, working under floodlights.

"Where do you want to start?" Paul asked her.

"The vehicles. Let's take a look at Evan's rental while the police are concentrating on Miller's car."

They walked over to the sedan, and Kendra studied the exterior. "The police will want to extract the two rounds that struck the door, but let's check out the interior."

Kendra put on a pair of latex gloves, then slipped behind the driver's seat and looked around. While she flipped down visors and looked in the center console, Paul checked the glove compartment.

"We need something brighter than the dome light that's in here," he said. "Let me borrow something from the crime scene van."

As Paul strode away, Kendra saw Evan's hard-sided rifle case still lying on the back seat cushion. Beside it was a leather portfolio. Under the circumstances, looking inside for his notes seemed like a good idea. Maybe Evan had left a copy of a memo or correspondence that would reveal who else knew of his travel plans.

It was unlocked, and Kendra brought out several folders. The first was a file on a case she wasn't involved in, so she set it down. The next folder turned out to be a copy of her marshal service personnel file.

Kendra skimmed the top page, and as she did she felt a coldness envelope her. Evan's latest recommendation was that she be removed from the field entirely and reassigned to desk or training duty permanently. Anger filled her. He'd never believed she was being tailed, but with an informant still in place, things would continue to get worse.

As she glanced at Paul and saw the resolve etched on his face she knew that, like her, he was in this to the end. No matter how tough things got, Paul would remain beside her until they completed what had to be done.

Chapter Eighteen

Once she'd finished checking the interior of Evan's sedan, Kendra went to the crime scene van to look at the items removed from Miller's car. The first thing she did, still wearing latex gloves, was remove the cell phone from the evidence bag.

It seemed odd to her that Miller had chosen a smart phone instead of a cheap throwaway. Something like this could be traced, even if it had been stolen, as she suspected it had been.

She turned on the phone, but there were no saved names or numbers, only a huge collection of apps that came with the device. Seeing an unfamiliar icon among the rest, she activated it with a touch.

Kendra realized almost instantly what it was. Hurrying out of the van, she signaled Paul. "Miller has a GPS app on his phone, and it's indicating this location. See if there's a GPS sender in Evan's car somewhere."

"They're making them smaller and smaller these days, so it may take a while. Let me check the typical hiding places first." Paul walked around the car, checking the easily accessed wheel wells, and stopped as he reached the rear.

"I've got something." He pulled out a device the size of a pocket calculator and showed it to her. "Here's the tracker. It was glommed in place with what feels like rubber cement. Didn't Miller have a tube of that stuff in his car?"

"Yeah, but how on earth did Miller know which rental car Evan would be using? That sedan isn't from the motor pool."

She paused. "I'm going to have Preston get a warrant so we can access Miller's complete call record-and another one to search his room, when we find where he's been staying." She placed Miller's phone back in the evidence bag and added her initials and the time to the tag.

"I'll call my brother for you," Paul said, but before he could dial, Preston pulled up. "That son of a gun has his own built-in radar. Even when we were kids, he was like that. Whenever I needed him, there he was."

"Maybe that's part of the gift that comes from his fetish. Yours is lynx. What's Preston's?" she asked.

Paul shook his head. "That's his secret to share—not mine."

As Preston joined them, Paul showed him what they'd found.

"Thomas picked up the rental car at a lot right across from the Hartley airport," Preston said, "so Miller must have arrived first and attached it, or he had an accomplice waiting and watching. Maybe the tracker was put there in case Thomas decided to change his destination. That way Miller could set up another shot."

"It helped that Evan wasn't on his guard and didn't spot the placement of the GPS. He also ignored my reports and refused to believe there was a problem," she said, then told him about the personnel file she'd found.

"If you hadn't stood your ground and fired back at the shooter, Thomas might be dead right now. I'll be happy to remind him of that for you," Paul said.

She barely managed to conceal a smile. Paul was a fiercely loyal, unwavering ally, and that was one of the things she loved most about him.

She'd never met a man quite like Paul. In his arms, she'd found both gentleness and strength waiting for her. His touch could make her burn with passion, or soothe her, if that's what she needed. That calm steadiness that came from his unflagging courage continued to draw her to him.

Kendra took a breath and forced herself to focus on the case. "Do you have anything new for us, Preston?" she asked.

"Yeah, as a matter of fact, I do. I found out where Miller was staying, a motel not far from here. That's now named in the search warrant. It's my next stop, and I thought you'd want to come with me and take a look around."

"You bet," she said without hesitation.

With Preston in the lead car, they made their way southeast across Hartley.

"We're close to finding the answers," she said softly. "Can you feel it?"

He nodded. "Yeah. It's something that starts in your gut, then all your senses become fine-turned. Smell, taste, everything becomes super sharp. There's no other feeling like it. Well, maybe one."

She laughed. "Stay on track. Even with Miller sidelined, we've never been in more danger. Whoever hired Miller will throw everything he's got at us now."

"I know."

"There's something I need to do." She took a long, deep breath. "If we run into trouble, you'll need the authority to act in an official capacity, using deadly force if necessary. I have special deputation authority, so I'd like to swear you in."

"All right," he said with a nod.

"As soon as we get to the motel, we'll make it official," she said.

Ten minutes later they arrived at an upscale motel at the junction of two main city streets that merged onto the highway leading out of Hartley. The five-story building was roughly stuccoed with a Mediterranean look that included balconies and a red slate roof. The landscaping was immaculate, even for this time of year, and a sign proclaimed the presence of an indoor pool, sauna and gym.

"Guess Miller doesn't like to rough it," she said.

"In his shoes I wouldn't have stayed in a cheap dump either. Those attract low-end criminals, generate trouble and, ultimately, the police. Here, the room rates alone guarantee him more privacy."

Once out of the car, Kendra saw Preston parked just ahead, talking on his radio. While he finished his business, she stood before Paul. "Are you ready to be sworn in?"

"Absolutely."

"Raise your right hand. Do you solemnly swear to faithfully execute the duties of a U.S. Marshal, so help you God?"

"I do," he said, his voice strong and clear. Something in the tone made Kendra realize just how much he still missed his old job.

"It's like a step back in time for you, isn't it? I'm—" She started to say she was sorry, but the last thing Paul wanted was her sympathy. She fell into an uneasy silence.

"I do miss the job," he said, "but I meant it when I said I wouldn't go back even if I could. When I first started my business, I saw it as a temporary thing, something to keep me distracted while I sorted myself out, but I've made a place for myself in Hartley. Now that Grayhorse Investigations is turning a steady profit, I'm going to accept the offer Daniel made me when I first opened my agency's doors. He wanted to merge our companies and make it a family-owned business. I didn't jump in back then because I didn't feel I was bringing enough to the table, at least in comparison to him, but he said he'd be ready whenever I was. Now I am."

"It sounds perfect, you two working together," she said. "It would also broaden your options, wouldn't it?"

"Yeah," he said with a smile. "I'd get to do more field work, which is something I've wanted."

Preston stood by the side door and waved. "You two coming, or taking a vacation?"

Paul laughed. "Let's go."

A few minutes later they entered a large, ground-floor room close to the rear exit of the main structure. "Fancy model laptop," Preston said, glancing at the corner desk across from them.

Kendra walked across the thick carpet, then stopped and studied the computer without touching it. "This could have information that'll lead us to whoever hired Miller. I'd like to take a quick look." Seeing Preston nod, she turned it on with a gloved hand.

As they waited for the computer to boot up, she helped Paul and Preston search the room. In the closet were two gun cases, one with two nine millimeter autoloader pistols and spare, loaded magazines, and the other containing a .308 caliber bolt action Remington rifle with fifty rounds of hunting ammunition. There were also several small pistol and rifle targets, a hunting knife, New Mexico large game hunting flyers and two forest service maps of area woodlands.

Kendra noticed the hunting jacket and red vest on a hanger in the closet. "With deer season coming up, no one around here would have questioned all this stuff."

Kendra returned to the computer screen and tried to access the files, but kept getting an enter password screen. "It's encrypted. I can't get in without risking triggering a program that'll wipe everything clean," she said at last. "Do either of you know anyone who can hack into this thing?"

"Daniel," Preston and Paul said at once.

"Your brother's a computer geek?" she said.

"That's not how he'd express it, but, yeah, you bet," Paul said. "He's also got some top-notch techs on his payroll."

"The fewer people involved, the better," she said. "Did you happen to include an electronic device search on that warrant of yours, Preston?"

"Sure did. With today's criminal element, it's almost automatic when we conduct a search. And there's no problem using Daniel. The Hartley P.D. hires him all the time to do specialized work, so it's mostly a matter of getting the right signatures on the paperwork."

"This should have gone to the marshals service directly, but without knowing the good guys from the bad, I don't want to risk it," Kendra said. "I've got to think outside the box now."

Preston reached for the computer, but just then his cell phone rang. He took a step back, spoke hurriedly, then hung up. "Miller's awake," he said. "The doc says we can question him, but not for long. Supervisory Inspector Thomas is already out of recovery and has been moved into a private room."

"Miller's a target now, and with an informant on the inside, his employer may already know where he's at," Kendra said. "We have to move him to a secure location before all hell breaks loose."

"Here's what I can do," Preston said. "If his doctor consents, we can move Miller to a small but well-equipped clinic on the Rez. I've got a place already in mind. I'll tell only a few key people, including my boss, and keep the relocation under wraps that way."

"He's my prisoner. I have to be in on the transfer," Kendra said.

"All right. I'll set it up. Where will you two be sleeping ?" Preston asked.

"I hadn't thought that far ahead," Kendra said.

"I have an idea. You're both still in the crosshairs, and I'm betting neither of you has had a good night's sleep in days," Preston said. "I know a place where you'll be safe. The Wilson brothers have a large, secure house. One's a former cop, and the other two are currently with the department. They let us use the place whenever we have a high threat situation. It's strictly for emergencies, but you'll have two cops keeping watch, plus George."

"George Wilson went blind after an accident and was forced to retire, right?" Paul said.

"Yeah, but he can hear someone breathing at twenty-five yards. In the dark he's more aware than either you or me."

"Refocused senses. It works that way sometimes." Paul

glanced at Kendra. "George's brothers, Jake and Hank, could bench press a horse, too. Those guys are *big*."

"No one messes with them," Preston said, "but you two won't be able to use the same room. The Wilsons are very straitlaced about things like that."

"I remember. Their dad's a preacher," Paul said, then added, "I see no problem with that. They've always shown respect for Navajo ways, and I can do the same for theirs."

"Me, too," Kendra said. "Give us the address."

THERE WAS A big iron gate at the walled entrance to the Wilson home, but as Paul and Kendra drove up, it swung open to the inside and Paul was able to drive in without stopping. Their headlights soon swept past an enormous, blue-uniformed cop standing on the far side of the covered porch.

"Talk about security, it's barely four in the morning and they've already got someone outside. Which of the brothers is he?" Kendra asked.

"That's Hank. He must have been pulled off duty." Paul parked his pickup next to a Hartley patrol car. "Come on. I'll introduce you," he said, stepping down from the truck as the gate clanked shut behind them.

When Hank came up to meet them, flashlight in hand, Kendra suddenly realized just how big he really was. Paul was over six feet tall, but Hank Wilson was half a head taller, and must have weighed two fifty. He was the kind of backup someone like her would have wanted when walking into a Denver biker bar. If Hank had played sports, she could easily imagine him as a defensive end.

Paul bumped fists with Hank, then introduced Kendra.

"Pleased to meet you, ma'am," Hank said, his voice almost soft despite the deep tone. "It's all copacetic out here at the moment. I'll be watching the grounds but I'll try not to make any noise. You two don't have to worry. Just catch up on your sleep, okay?"

"Thanks. Jake and George inside?" Paul asked.

"Copy that. Just ring the bell when you go to the door, okay? Anyone who knocks gets a pistol waved in their face."

"Good to know," Kendra said. "Nice to meet you, Hank."

"You too, ma'am. Good night."

As they stepped up onto the porch, Kendra waited while Paul reached for the doorbell. "If the other brothers are like Hank, they're really on the ball. And polite," she added with a smile.

The door opened just a crack, and they both turned at the sound. "Preston?" a deep voice asked.

"No, Paul and Marshal Armstrong," Paul said, noting Kendra's puzzled reaction.

"Just testing to make sure everything's okay. Come on in, you two," Jake said, opening the door. As they stepped in, the man, maybe an inch shorter than Hank, placed his handgun back into his holster.

"I'm Jake, Shorty to my brothers," he said with a smile, nodding to Paul, then offering his massive hand to Kendra.

"I'm Kendra, Kendra Armstrong. Thanks so much for your hospitality on such short notice, Jake," she said, surprised by the gentleness of his handshake.

"Pleased to be of help, ma'am," Jake said. "Make yourself at home. You two will be as safe as babies tonight."

"Appreciate your help," Paul said, looking around at the big room. The overstuffed chairs and two sofas in the living room were arranged in a half circle around a cozy, blazing pellet stove a few feet from a brick wall. Mounted on the wall itself was a big screen TV, and against another wall were a digital music center and wooden shelves with CDs.

"Thought I heard a racket," a soft, pleasant voice called from the kitchen side of the room. Kendra turned and saw the oldest giant of the Wilson brothers. George wore shaded glasses and picked his way past a massive oak table and chairs with certainty.

"Would you two like something to eat? I'm a good cook, if I say so myself. When you can't see, taste becomes more important."

"Actually, I'm beat. If you don't mind, I'd rather call it a night, or morning, I guess, and get some sleep," she said.

"Sure." George led the way down a short hall, then opened the door.

There'd been no hesitation. "You knew precisely where the door and the knob would be," Kendra said, surprised.

"I know this house like my own heartbeat. I can tell when something doesn't sound right, or if anything's been taken away or added to any of the rooms," George said. "If anyone's outside beside my brothers, I'll know that, too, maybe even before Hank and Jake. When blindness took away my sight, the good Lord gave me other gifts."

"This room is great. Thank you," Kendra said, glancing around.

"Clean sheets, fresh towels. If you need anything else, just call. I won't be far."

"Thanks," Kendra said. "There is one thing. I'll need to be up at eight. Is there an alarm clock?"

"Jake will knock on your door at that time," George said.

"Great. Then we're all set."

As the men left, Kendra sat down on the edge of the king-sized bed. This could be the last night she'd be working with Paul. The thought felt like a heavy weight over her heart. She hadn't come to Hartley wanting, or even hoping, to fall in love, but her heart had made other plans.

After undressing down to her underwear, she crawled beneath the covers and switched off the light.

Despite her exhaustion, for a long while all she could do was stare into the dark. Everything inside her hurt. She didn't want to go back to her empty apartment in Denver, then try to tell herself that Mr. Right didn't exist. He did—he'd just come with pre-existing conditions.

Paul couldn't give her his whole heart, and even if she could have accepted it for herself, it wasn't fair to the family she'd eventually have. When it came to love and family, it was all or nothing.

With silent tears running down her face, she gradually faded into a deep, dreamless sleep.

SHORTLY AFTER BREAKFAST they left the Wilsons' home and headed to the hospital. Things were already well underway there, and soon, they were ready to transport Miller.

Two vehicles pulled out of the ambulance port, a sheltered bay that provided quick access to the emergency room. Preston and another officer led the way in a large black SUV with tinted windows. Paul followed, driving the ambulance, with Kendra at his side.

Kendra wore a protective vest, and the short barrel of a shotgun rested between her feet, visible to anyone who passed by on the passenger side of the ambulance in a high-profile truck or van.

"This time of the morning we won't be facing much traffic. Most of the coal mine and power plant employees have already changed shifts," Paul said.

"We've got a good plan, and even if we do draw fire, we have the advantage. They'll assume Miller's with us and that'll buy your brother time to get him away safely. I only wish we could have had an escort behind us, as well, but Preston's right. It would have looked like a VIP motorcade and attracted too much attention."

Soon they were rolling down the four-lane highway ten minutes west of Hartley. Traffic flow and bad timing forced them to stop at a light in the small community of Kirtland, just north of the Navajo Nation boundary. It was the last stop before Shiprock, a dozen or so miles farther west. Traffic was heavier here than before, but their small convoy stayed together.

Paul checked the rearview mirror. "There's a white van be-hind us. It's probably a service or utility vehicle, but I can't see a company or agency name from this angle."

"There are two men inside wearing baseball caps and big shades. We've got the sun at our backs, and that makes the use of shades a bit odd. They look more like spooks than any-thing else," Kendra said.

Kendra checked out the new-looking pickup that pulled up beside them at the light. There were two men in the cab there, also wearing ball caps and sunglasses. "To my right," she said, "another pair of spooks in heavy jackets."

Paul looked over. "Something's not right. They're not the least bit curious about us."

"Yeah, and here we are in this ambulance."

As the light changed, Preston's SUV surged ahead. Paul accelerated to keep up, but suddenly the pickup beside them veered into their lane.

"Hang on!" Paul swerved the heavy ambulance to the left, lessening a blow to the right front bumper, but the ambulance still shook hard on impact. As he pulled the wheel back to the right, he caught the pickup's rear bumper as it tried to cut them off. The truck fishtailed, almost catching an oncoming car, then straightened out, rocketing ahead.

"Behind us!" Kendra grabbed the dashboard.

The white van slammed into them with a bone-jarring thud. Kendra bounced forward, but the seat belt kept her from hit-ting the windshield.

Paul looked ahead. The passenger of the pickup was lean-ing out his window, pointing a gun. "Duck!"

A bullet shattered the windshield, striking the rearview mirror, which broke loose and bounced off the back of the cab. Paul tried to hold the wheel steady, but the van hit them again on the right rear bumper and sent them skittering down the highway, tires screaming. Paul yanked the wheel to the right, avoiding an end-over-end rollover.

Kendra drew her gun as the van pulled up on her side, but it instantly dropped back into their blind spot.

Paul yanked out his pistol, back in control of the ambulance, but by then the pickup was speeding away. The van behind them cut its speed, whipped across the median, and also raced off.

"What the hell?" Paul looked at Kendra. "They had us pinned. Why did they bail?"

Kendra looked out the side mirror. "There's something stuck on our side panel back there. Get off the road, fast! There, that empty lot," she said, pointing.

Ten seconds later, she leaped out of the cab and took a quick look at the object.

"Bomb!" she yelled to Paul. "Run!"

They were barely twenty feet away when the blast shook the ground. Enveloped in a wave of heat and pressure, they were thrown forward onto the gravel.

"You okay?" Paul said.

"Yeah," she said, coughing.

They rose to their feet slowly and turned to watch the mass of flames that covered the ambulance. Billowing black smoke rose upwards in dark waves.

Paul looked over at Kendra. "You can bet they're watching us with binoculars right now and think they killed Miller."

"Good thing Miller's safe and sound in Preston's SUV."

"We bought some time, that's all," Paul warned.

"It may be a small win, but it's one that counts."

Daniel, his head out the window, pulled up in a second SUV, this one blue. "Come on. Get in!"

Paul and Kendra didn't hesitate. "What are *you* doing here?" Paul asked, waving Kendra in first. "I never told—"

Daniel gunned the engine the second they were both inside. "Preston asked me to cover the move but stay well behind so I wouldn't be made. When I saw you running from the ambulance, I figured out what was going down. Now let's get out of here."

Forty-five minutes later they arrived at a reservation clinic south of Beclabito in the piñon/juniper hills. Preston was outside waiting for them.

Kendra looked around. "Good choice. No way to sneak up on this place. There's not much cover around here."

"That, and we're thirty miles deep on the Rez so a white man sticks out like a sore thumb," Preston said, leading the way inside. "One good thing—the bomb attack rattled our prisoner. He wants to cut a deal—immunity in exchange for his testimony."

"He killed a U.S. Marshal and Annie Crenshaw. Those defensive scratches found on his arms are going to seal a conviction when the DNA under Annie's fingernails comes back from the state lab. His only hope is a life sentence," Paul growled.

"Yes, but to survive even behind bars he'll need our help. That's going to be our leverage," Kendra said. "Of course *any* deal will be up to the federal prosecutor."

As they went down the short hallway, the doctor who'd ridden with Miller and Preston came out of a room to meet them. "Miller can be questioned whenever you're ready," he said, "but I'm going to stay in the room, monitoring his vitals, just in case there's a problem."

"Hold that thought, doc." Kendra took Preston aside. "How carefully did you vet out this doctor?"

"I'd trust him with my life. He's with the New Mexico National Guard and was wounded during a mortar attack on his medivac unit in Iraq. I chose him because I knew he could handle himself under fire."

"Okay." Kendra nodded to the doctor, then went inside the treatment room where Chris Miller lay on a hospital bed.

"You ready to cut me a deal?" Miller asked as Kendra came in. "I've got plenty to trade."

"Give me something big to take to the prosecutor, then we'll see what we can offer you." Kendra brought out her digital recorder and set it on the table next to the bed. After recording the date and time, she gave Miller a nod. "Okay, make it good."

Chapter Nineteen

Kendra waited as Miller sipped some water. He was taking his time. She wasn't sure if he wanted to back out or if he was just playing them.

"First, let me make one thing clear," Miller said at last. "I was hired to wound—not kill—your supervisor, Thomas."

"What?" Kendra sat up abruptly.

"You heard me," Miller said. "I was shown a photo, given the address, then ordered to make the hit once he got out of the car. I was paid to target an arm or leg—no head or torso shots."

Kendra shook her head in disbelief. "What a minute. Are you telling me that your client told you specifically *not* to kill Thomas?"

"Yeah. I was instructed to use a pistol caliber round with a full metal jacket. Less damage if it went through and through," he said. "It didn't matter to me, I got paid the same. But I was set up, too. I was told to expect one fed inside the house and the target, not a full security team."

"Your bad luck," Preston said. "How long have you been in town?"

Kendra knew he was trying to tie Miller to the earlier events.

Miller shook his head. "That's all I'm saying for now. What I've given you is just a taste of what's to come. Give me immunity—in writing—and we'll talk again."

"Were you responsible for the hit on Deputy Marshal Armstrong and Paul Grayhorse a few days ago?" Preston said, pressuring him anyway. "And the murder of Annie Crenshaw?"

"I'm only copping to a single charge of assault with a deadly weapon. The more you give me, the more I'll give you."

"Not good enough. Tell us who hired you," Preston said.

When Miller looked away and stared at the wall, Kendra stood and gestured toward the door.

Outside in the hall Preston glared at her. "That guy's playing us."

"Yeah, but he's got information to trade, and we need him," she said.

"All right then. I'll get in touch with the prosecutor," Preston said.

It took another hour and a half, but once they convinced Miller he'd be given protection behind bars and a new identity to protect him from hostile inmate retaliation, he relaxed.

"Okay, let's have it," Kendra said, staring her prisoner down.

"We're still talking *one* crime—the one where I winged Thomas. But here's something you didn't know. I was also hired to take you and the former marshal out permanently the moment the opportunity presented itself. Last night, today, tomorrow—ASAP. That was my next gig."

"So we were both targets," Kendra said quietly.

"My primary target was Thomas. You two were B-list."

Kendra didn't answer. "Now on to the big question. Who hired you for the job, Miller?"

He shrugged, then his lip curled into what might have been a smile. "I never ask for a name. That makes clients uneasy. But there's a way you can track him down. The carbine, clips loaded with ammo, and smart phone were all left for me at a prearranged location inside a discarded dog food bag and a paper sack. In the bottom of the sack, which contained everything except for the carbine, I found a sales slip for a cash transaction dated the day prior to my arrival, exactly one week ago. It wasn't for the stuff I picked up, but the name of the place was Roy's Happy Trigger."

"That's a gun shop on Hartley's west side just off the old highway," Paul said, looking at Kendra. "The owner's a good man, and even better, he's got a great security system. I provide it for him."

"Do you still have the receipt?" Kendra asked Miller, thinking of fingerprints.

"No, I threw it out."

Kendra stood. "We'll be back," she said.

"Wait a minute. Where's the protection I was promised?" Miller said. "One cop at the door isn't going to do it, you know."

"You're safe here," Preston said. "You'll have at least two armed guards outside 24/7, and others you'll never see. Considering your location, no one's going to sneak up either."

A few minutes later, after warning the doctor not to trust Miller, Kendra led the way back outside. "I want to talk to that Hartley gun shop owner as soon as possible."

"You two will have better luck if I'm not there," Preston said. "The proprietor and I have had our differences."

"That's because you keep telling him how to run his business," Paul said.

"All I've been suggesting is that he move his store out of that high crime neighborhood."

"So why's he staying there? You think he's involved in some shady side business, dealing illegal arms or something?" Kendra asked.

"No, it's not like that," Paul said. "Willie's dad started the gun shop and Willie doesn't want to move away and leave all his memories behind. When he looks around the neighborhood, he still sees it as it used to be, not run down like it is now."

Kendra was touched by the empathy in Paul's voice, a man

with more than his fair share of memories that continued to haunt him.

She didn't comment until they were back in Gene's truck, heading to Hartley. "I feel for Willie, but wanting things to stay the same..." She shook her head. "That's a losing battle."

"Sameness.... There was a time in my life when I would have considered that a curse of major proportions."

"Is that also part of the reason you've decided to accept Daniel's offer now? You want to stir things up a bit so the business will remain a challenge to you?"

"Yeah," he said with a smile. "Something like that. What about you? Are you ready for new challenges? If someone offered you a job with a decent salary and more regular hours, would you leave the marshals service and become a mom?"

She took a slow, deep breath. "It's not that simple. Salary's important and so are the hours, but there are other holdbacks I've yet to work out. For one, I don't have an extended family like yours who lives close by and could help me if I got sick or injured. I would also need to provide my child with some male role models, ones who would be around for more than an occasional birthday or holiday."

"Here's a thought. Come work for Daniel and me. You've got the training and skills we need, and I'll be close by and able to help you out if you're in a pinch."

She suspected that even a partial commitment like that one had been hard for Paul. He was a man who didn't open his heart easily to anyone outside his band of brothers. Yet halfway propositions weren't for her, and what he was offering just wasn't enough.

Paul was the kind of man she'd always dreamed of but never thought she'd find. When the going got rough, he'd remained right by her side. Yet although he was a relentless fighter, he could also show compassion.

Maybe those qualities also explained why Paul had been such an extraordinary lover. He was wildly passionate, yet he also knew how to take his time and prolong a woman's pleasure.

Paul had claimed a piece of her heart. When the time came for her to leave, she'd go, but the memories they'd carved out would be part of her forever.

THEY RODE IN silence until they reached their destination. "There's Willie's shop, straight ahead on the right side of the street," Paul said.

Kendra saw a small building ahead with bars on all the windows. The stores on both sides were closed and boarded up, but Roy's Happy Trigger seemed to attract a large volume of customers. The parking lot in front had just one empty space. "Looks like Willie's got a booming business."

"Yeah, he sure does. After his dad died, he inherited a shop that barely made ends meet. Willie turned it around and made it a huge success," Paul said. "He sees things differently, though. If you compliment him on the good job he's done, he'll just say that his dad did most of the hard work. He just improved a few things because that was what his dad expected him to do."

"Will he be leaving the place to his son?"

"Doesn't look like it. Willie says that he's married to the store. According to him, he's never even had time for dating."

"He sounds lonely, trapped."

He shook his head. "No, I don't think so. Willie just likes the status quo. By building up his business, he's honored his father's memory and found financial security. He has no desire to change anything."

"So rather than move locations and take a risk, he settles for the known."

He didn't answer right away. "Maybe. You know, sometimes it's hard to deal with memories that won't let go."

SINCE PAUL AND Willie already knew each other, Kendra asked Paul to take the lead. As they walked through the front door, ringing a small, overhead bell, Paul waved at the middle-aged man with the thinning hair and neatly trimmed beard. He was busy showing a hunting rifle to a customer.

"Just take a look around, folks," Willie called out without really looking up. "I'll be with you just as soon as we're done here."

Paul walked around, glancing at the shop displays as he waited. He'd taken his shot by asking Kendra to stay. He'd also been careful not to attach any strings to the arrangement or burden either of them with a slew of expectations.

Maybe if he'd had a different kind of life, he would have just gone for it, hoping for the best. That's what most people did, wasn't it?

What had held him back was knowing that she wanted to adopt. As someone who'd gone through the system, he knew firsthand how vulnerable kids who'd known rejection really were. If things didn't work out between Kendra and him, the same kind of scars he'd borne all his life could be imprinted on another child.

Happily-ever-after wasn't a concept he could believe in, so walking away had been his only logical option. He wouldn't make Kendra and the kids who'd come into their lives a promise he suspected belonged only in a fairy tale.

Paul tried to show some interest in a display of collectible infantry rifles from World War II, but his mind remained elsewhere.

Willie, apparently finished with his previous customer, came up to him. "Hey, buddy. What brings you in here before lunch? Are you going to pitch me a new upgrade to your surveillance system?"

Paul shook his head. "My lady friend and I need to talk to you privately," he said, catching Kendra's eye and motioning her over.

Willie waved to a clerk, then led them behind the counter to an office in the back of the shop. The small, windowless room

held a wooden desk, two small LED monitors and several filing cabinets. There were three chairs, one on casters with a
padded seat, and the other two, old-style metal folding chairs.

"My dad never liked white-collar offices. He said they
made a man soft," Willie said, smiling at Kendra as she came
in just behind Paul. "Now tell me what brings you two here.
From your expressions, I gather it's serious."

Paul gave him a quick update on what Miller had told them,
then showed Willie a photo of Miller's carbine.

Willie sat as still as a rock. "Dammit, you know I'm not
responsible for what people do with the guns they buy here. I
run the mandatory background check, and if the buyer comes
back clean, I finalize the purchase."

"Relax, Willie, we know that," Paul assured him quickly.
"The reason we came is that we need your help to track down
this guy. The cameras will have a record of all your customers and we're hoping to find a familiar face."

He nodded. "Okay, have at it, while I go check my records
and get the names of our cash customers for that day."

Seeing two more customers come in, Willie looked at Paul.
"Give me another few minutes. Matt needs my help out there.
You know where everything is, so go ahead and access the
feed. Let me know if you find the guy you want. If it's someone I deal with regularly, I may be able to tell you where to
find him."

As he left, Paul sat down at the desk and pulled back the
keyboard stand. There was a mouse beside it and the proper
monitor came out of sleep mode in a few seconds.

It took Paul a few minutes, but the feed soon began. "The
images are pretty clear, and since the camera's not readily
visible, no one bothers to turn away."

"Nice touch."

"Thanks," he said. "The surveillance business can seem
really tame after working the field, but it provides tangible
results. Willie used to get held up three or four times a year.

Since the cameras went in and the stickers went up on the windows six months ago, he's had one robbery and the suspect was identified and arrested within a day."

"You don't always need a gun to fight crime. The right information is often all that's needed for the bad guys to get caught and the public to win."

"Navajos call it restoring the balance. That's how we walk in beauty."

"It's a good way to look at it," she said. "To me, what's always been important isn't the star or badge that comes with the job, it's the work itself."

"Does that mean you're considering joining our family business?"

"You're making it sound like the Mafia!" she said, chuckling but not answering his question.

"You've been in the city too long," he said, smiling.

Kendra, who'd focused on the screen, suddenly sat up. "Stop! Freeze that frame." Even though he was wearing a hat and sunglasses, she knew exactly who the man in the video was. Her body grew cold as she realized the magnitude of that one man's betrayal. "I can't believe this. He fooled everyone—including me."

Chapter Twenty

"Evan Thomas, my boss," Kendra said softly. "He knew we were getting close to catching Miller, so he arranged to get himself shot, knowing it would keep him in the clear a while longer."

"He was probably also hoping that we'd end up killing Miller. That would have practically guaranteed that his connection to the cartel would have never come to light," Paul said.

"I have a feeling we're right on all counts, but we still have a problem. The hat and sunglasses obscure too much of his face. I know that's Evan, but a defense attorney could successfully throw out my ID. The word of a professional hit man that led us to the buy isn't going to get us a conviction either. If Miller never saw him, Evan could weasel out of this in any of a thousand ways. We need more evidence," Kendra said.

"Agreed, but we're going to have to watch our step. If I'm right, Evan's been undermining operations for a while. Evan was my supervisor, and I'm beginning to suspect that one of his first jobs was setting up Judy and me. After Judy's...end of watch..." he said, using their service's term for the deceased, "I heard about other ops that went wrong. They blamed it on a lot of things, including mistakes by the marshals in charge, but I believe the pattern began back then."

Willie returned, took a look at both of them and smiled. "You got what you wanted, I see." He held up a piece of paper.

"Matt, my clerk, made the sale. Here's the name of the buyer and an address. I've also got the serial number of the weapon he purchased, a nine millimeter Ruger carbine I picked up third-hand via an estate sale. I've also written down the name of the supplier, a friend of mine who shops for guns at estate sales and gets some great deals."

Kendra took the paper and held it so she and Paul could both read the note. "Right serial number, but not the right name for the purchaser. His ID was fake. Evan prepared something gathered from a federal database, my guess, or it wouldn't have passed background."

"Doesn't matter now. We got our lead." Paul looked at Willie. "I need to borrow one of your flash drives so I can make a copy of the footage. I'd also like to use your computer to email the image on that frame to Daniel."

"Do whatever you need," Willie said.

Less than five minutes later, Kendra and Paul were on their way across town. "Paul, I have to ask you something. Is your past connection to this case going to be a problem?"

"You think I want to catch up to Evan so I can blow him away?"

"No, that's not it at all. You live by certain rules, just like me. That's what makes us the good guys."

He reached for her hand, then brought it up to his lips. "I'm glad you believe in me."

"I do, but I also need to know that you'll play this by the book—no short cuts just to achieve the goal."

"We can do that, but we'll still have to push Evan hard," Paul said. "I say we confront him with the video and the sales record. Let him know that you're taking the information up the chain of command. Then we'll watch and see what he does. My guess is that he'll damn himself one way or another."

"Evan's not stupid, quite the opposite. How else to explain how he's managed to stay under the radar for so long?" she said. "He'll know we've got nothing that'll stick."

"Matt, the gun shop clerk, may be able to positively ID Evan as the customer who bought the carbine," he said.

"Or not."

"We have the serial number on that weapon," Paul said.

"That identifies the weapon, but we still can't conclusively tie that to Evan. We need to *prove* he was the purchaser and that he turned that gun over to Miller. Our biggest problem is that Miller never saw his client—Evan."

"Let's tell Evan that Preston is questioning Miller right now and that Miller's claiming he's got a source inside the marshals service. We won't be accusing Evan of anything, but we'll be pointing out a problem that Evan may see as a direct threat. Then we'll hang back and see what Evan's next move is," Paul said.

"All right. We'll do it that way, and see what he does."

It didn't take Kendra long to find Thomas. He'd checked out of the hospital and was back in his Hartley motel room. "Before we go over there, we need to get a reliable tracking device. We don't want to lose Evan if he makes a run for it."

"He'll be on the lookout for that. He'll probably search his luggage and whatever vehicle he's got to make sure they're clean and stay that way," Paul said.

"That's why I want to use *two* devices—one that he'll find after a careful search and another he won't expect."

"Daniel can help us with that," Paul said, and reached for his cell.

By the time they arrived at Daniel's place he was waiting and ushered them inside quickly. "I've got what you asked for, and actually got you a third device so you can game the gamer," he said.

"Thanks," Kendra said. "I like it. We'll put one where he'll be sure to find it, then place the second somewhere he'll have to search hard to find. When he finally spots it, he'll assume he's outsmarted us and he's good to go. He'll never look for a third."

"Nice use of game theory," Paul said.

"Are you sure you don't want backup on this?" Daniel asked Paul, then glanced at Kendra.

"No. We have to give Evan plenty of room," she said. "If he senses a trap, he has all the training necessary to disappear for good. I'm sure he's got stashes of cash and identities he can assume at a moment's notice."

Paul checked out the three small devices. "You can plant the smallest one on him, Kendra. He won't be expecting that. I'll take the other two and put one inside the wheel well of his car, a place he's bound to check, and another in his gear."

"Okay, let's get rolling then." Kendra dialed the hotel and got Thomas after three rings.

Though it was difficult, she kept her voice steady and businesslike. "Miller's in custody," she said. "The local P.D. is questioning him now. Miller has told them that he's working with a partner inside the marshals service, but we don't have a name yet."

"Where's he being held? He's not in the hospital. I checked," Thomas said.

"For his own protection, I had him moved to an Arizona clinic," she said, deliberately misleading him. "He's still under heavy guard."

"You shouldn't have acted without my knowledge," Thomas snapped.

"It's my case—my fugitive."

"It *was* your case. Now it's mine." He stopped short, then, after a moment, continued. "Get over here. We'll talk about the evidence you've gathered and see where the case stands."

KENDRA AND PAUL arrived at the motel ten minutes later and went directly to Thomas's room.

Kendra sat on one of the chairs placed by a round table near the window.

"The evidence is sketchy, Evan," she said. "We have the

name of the gun shop where the carbine and ammunition were purchased. The purchaser didn't notice a receipt lodged under a flap in the paper bag, apparently. We pressed the business owner for more details but apparently one of his younger clerks made the sale and can't recall the buyer. The clerk is reviewing hours of video, so once he identifies the guy, we'll have more."

"Miller probably wasn't the one who bought the weapon and ammo, so you could be on a wild-goose chase."

"If his employer or partner provided Miller with what he needed for the hit, it's possible we'll recognize him once we view the feed."

Thomas stood, idly adjusted the sling on his wounded arm, and stared at an indeterminate spot across the room. Paul also remained standing, positioned beside Evan's carry-on bag, which was on the carpet, unzipped. "I've kept you out of the loop as long as possible, but now I don't have a choice. There are things you need to know, Kendra."

Thomas looked at Paul.

"He's been deputized," Kendra said, "if that helps."

Evan nodded. "What I'm about to say can't leave this room. Am I clear?" he said, looking at her, then at Paul.

"All right," Kendra said, then saw Paul also nod. He raised an eyebrow, as well, signaling that he'd deployed the first listening device. She guessed it had been tossed into Evan's open luggage.

Thomas had other things on his mind. "If Miller's talking, some of the things he'll say will eventually point back to me as his inside man. He's never seen my face, but if he made a recording of any of our conversations, voice identification software might also identify me."

"Are you admitting guilt?" Paul growled, taking a step closer to the supervisor.

Thomas held his ground. "You're off base, Grayhorse. I'm not the bad guy here."

"Yes you are." Paul moved like the wind, and in two seconds Thomas was pressed against the wall.

"You're interfering with a federal investigation, and you're going to blow my whole case. Back off—now," Thomas ordered, undaunted.

"What investigation?" Kendra forced herself between the two men, one hand on the back of Evan's collar and the other on Paul's forearm. "Back up, Paul."

Evan turned around. "I've been working undercover for nearly a year, worming my way into a criminal network that covers half the country."

"And selling out my partner and me was part of your job?" Paul snarled. "Nice try."

"What happened to you and your partner wasn't part of the plan," Thomas said. "That's the truth."

"I should be able to verify all this," Kendra said, picking up her phone. "Who's your department handler, Evan?"

"There's no way I can tell you that. I've got reason to suspect there's another informant in our office, one we've yet to unmask. Lives are at stake here, not just careers."

"So we're just supposed to believe this undercover story you're selling?" Paul said, moving in with clenched fists.

Kendra got in his way again, forcing Paul back.

"If you go off half-cocked, Paul, you'll destroy months of undercover work. Judy died at the hands of these jerks. Are you going to let it be for nothing?" Evan said, his eyes on Paul.

Paul lunged forward, his forearm at Thomas's neck, pinning him to the wall, but he avoided touching Evan's injured arm this time.

"Stop!" Kendra snapped. "Enough with the testosterone." She took hold of Paul's shoulder and eased him back again. "Let's sit down and reason this out."

Evan sat on the edge of the bed, then ran a hand through his close-cropped hair. "After the attempt on the judge that resulted in the death of Deputy Marshal Judy Whitacre, I began to suspect that the Hawthorn cartel had a well-placed informant in our office. We'd taken every precaution, yet they still managed to have a sniper in position to make the attempted hit."

"Did you report your suspicion?" Paul demanded.

"I had no evidence, and you don't bring up something like that unless you can make the case. To get the proof I needed I knew I'd have to go undercover," he said. "I eventually earned the cartel's confidence by passing along information, but it was always the kind I knew we could afford to lose."

"Like the fact that I was here in Hartley, and setting me up as Miller's next target?" Paul growled, his eyes cold and without expression.

"No. I never gave them your exact location. I also made sure you had one of our best marshals on the scene in case things got rough. That's the real reason I sent Kendra to retrieve Miller."

"You tried to discredit me when I reported that the cartel had an informant. Yet you knew I was right," she said.

"There was no way you could have accomplished what I could as an insider, so I protected my cover. All you would have done was get yourself killed, and you would have never even seen it coming. By sending you down here I gave you both a chance."

Paul stood, rock still, staring at Thomas. "You spin a nice story, I'll give you that, but it's nothing more than a skilled evasion unless we can verify it."

"Take a look at the facts. I never gave Miller your exact location, but he still found you. That proves the cartel has another well-placed source on the inside. Unless we ID that person, we're all in danger," Evan said. "My life is already on the line. The cartel suspects I've been playing them because my information is always missing key details. This is my last chance to finish what I've started."

"But if you've been compromised…" Kendra started, pointing to his arm.

"This wound is precisely why I'm still alive. I offered to take a bullet from the cartel's sniper. I convinced them that would help my credibility at the marshals service and allow me to continue to feed them information. That also proved my loyalty to the cartel since I was trusting them with my life," Evan said. "It was a calculated risk, of course, but I'll have more room to maneuver now and be able to penetrate deeper into their organization."

"You're asking me to trust you, but you've given me absolutely no proof of anything," Kendra said. "All I've got is your word."

"Do you really want to risk everything by sticking to protocol now?" Evan said. "I'm ready to make my move. Let me finish this."

"All right. I'm listening. What do you have in mind?" Kendra said.

"A large weapons stash is going to be shipped across the border into Mexico any day now. Garrett Hawthorne is going to be there himself to supervise the operation. If we raid the place today, we can prevent those guns from ever leaving the warehouse. We'll also be able to collar Garrett with enough evidence to put him away for life."

"Or we could be walking into a trap," Paul said.

Thomas looked at Paul, then back at her. "If I'd been working for the cartel, I could have taken either of you out long before now. I knew where you were and could have brought you into the open easily enough."

"Where's this warehouse?" Kendra asked after a beat.

"I don't know for sure yet, but it's local. I'm supposed to link up with one of Hawthorn's soldiers, get the location from him, and then go meet Garrett." Thomas checked his watch. "Crap, I'm already fifteen minutes late. I'm supposed to drive to Spencer's Superstore and meet him in the parking lot."

"Take one of us along," Paul said.

"No, that won't work. They don't like strangers, and they hate surprises of any kind." He paused for a few seconds, then continued. "What you *can* do is track me all the way via my cell phone's GPS. As soon as I get the warehouse's location, I'll text you with a quick single character, lower case k, as in okay. Stay out of the area until you get my signal, then make your move. Avoid using SWAT because their arrival is sure to tip off any spotters keeping watch on the neighborhood. Also, after it all goes down, make sure you take me prisoner along with the rest. That'll protect my cover."

PAUL WALKED OUT with Thomas while Kendra reported to Preston and brought him up to date.

"I'll deliver on this, don't worry," Thomas said.

As they reached the rented sedan, Paul suddenly grabbed Thomas and threw him against the driver's side front fender. "If you set us up, there'll be no place on earth where you can hide from me. I'll find you."

"If I'd wanted you dead, Grayhorse, you would have been a corpse already. Let me go."

Paul stepped back and allowed Thomas to get into the car.

As Paul turned to walk back to the motel, he wiped away the dust and road grime from the fingertips on his left hand. While roughing up Thomas and effectively distracting him, he'd used his free left hand to slip the second tracking device under the front tire well. The first one had been slipped into Thomas's luggage.

Thomas was bound to eventually find the two devices he'd planted, then probably ditch the electronics, including his phone. Depending on how prepared he was, Thomas might also end up abandoning the car he was currently driving.

The smallest, third device, the one they were counting on to track him, was planted in the back of his collar. Kendra had placed it there when they'd all been back in the room, and she'd stepped between Thomas and him, ostensibly to split them up.

After Thomas left, Kendra joined Paul and they were on their way moments later.

"Preston's ready?" he asked.

"Yeah. He'll wait for our call." She remained silent for several moments. "I don't trust Evan. Something about this feels…off."

"To me, too. It was almost too easy. His explanation was plausible, but it sounded too well rehearsed."

Paul stayed a half mile back, well out of visual range as they followed the three dots on the GPS screen targeting Thomas's location. "Do you have someone inside the marshals service you'd trust with your life?" he asked her.

She thought about it a moment, then nodded slowly. "Several, but one in particular, Tim Johnson. I was his partner for two years before he was relocated to Washington."

"A mover and shaker?" he said, pushing back the stab of jealousy. Had they been as close as Judy and him? A storm raged inside him as he thought of her with someone else.

"Tim demanded a lot from himself. Five minutes with him and you knew he was destined to climb the ladder."

"Is he the kind who goes strictly by the book?" he said, biting off each word.

"No, not really. He's more results oriented. What is it you want him to do?"

"The day Judy and I were shot, backup arrived within five minutes. Thomas showed up with the deputies who first came on the scene, too, though he wasn't part of their team. I never questioned it because, to me, he was one of the good guys. Now I'd like to know why he was in the area. You said he was your team's sniper?"

Kendra's mouth fell open, but she recovered quickly. "You think he was the one who tried to make the hit on the judge?"

"He showed up out of thin air, and if memory serves me, he

was on foot. Of course there was a lot of confusion, and I was flat on my back on the pavement at the time in a lot of pain."

"Was he part of your protection detail?" Kendra asked.

"No, but if he had official business in the area it should be on record somewhere," Paul said.

Kendra nodded. "Okay, I'll ask Tim to check that out for me. He won't hesitate."

Kendra made the call, and Paul heard her tone of voice change as she spoke to her former partner. She'd greeted Johnson like a friend, but the awkwardness that would sometimes result between former lovers—or partners who'd crossed that line—was absent. Still, it was clear that they liked each other and that irked him. He wanted her to get to the point quickly and end the conversation, but somehow held his peace.

An eternity later, she hung up. "He'll check."

"We've got another problem," Paul said, pointing to the screen. "Thomas ditched two of the bugs and his cell phone as I thought he would. The signals are coming from a strip mall ahead. The other bug, probably the one you stuck under his collar, has him heading north."

"I wonder if he's running to, or from, his cartel friends?"

"We'll find out soon enough," Paul answered. "Call Preston and fill him in, and ask officers to check the strip mall. I suspect Evan had a second vehicle stashed there. Under the circumstances, it makes sense that he'd want to ditch the sedan. We know what it looks like."

"If the tracker indicates he's heading out of the city or to the airport, we'll have to pick him up," Kendra said.

"I don't think he'll make a run for it," Paul said. "He'll probably go to ground somewhere after linking up with the cartel."

Kendra updated Preston, then, keeping him on the speaker phone, added, "Looks like Thomas circled Main Street twice, then stopped. He's moving so slowly now, he must be on foot."

"There's a dry cleaners there—Smith's Finest—that seems

to attract a lot of suspicious characters," Preston said. "We've been watching the place for weeks but we still don't have a clue what's really going on there."

"Tell us more about the cleaners," she said, glancing at Paul, who nodded.

"Hang on." They heard Preston sending an unmarked patrol unit to watch the cleaners, then seconds later, he returned to the phone. "It's a one-story cinder block building with a front entrance and one back exit into the alley."

"How about the roof? Any escape through there?" Kendra asked.

"A skylight, maybe, since it's a flat-roofed structure. We can have an officer cover that from the building next door," Preston said, then added, "But no way that's the warehouse Thomas told you about."

"I'm guessing that this is the first meet," Paul said. "Thomas will talk to one of Hawthorn's lieutenants and try to get the cartel's help leaving the country."

"Waiting around to see if he can lead us to bigger fish is too risky," Kendra said. "Evan's smart and knows how we work. Let's move now."

"You ready to make the arrest?" Preston asked.

"Ten-four," Kendra said.

Chapter Twenty-One

Ten minutes later Preston and several detectives entered the dry cleaners from the street. Kendra and Paul were positioned out back, weapons ready.

Within a few seconds a man wearing a suit jacket and slacks burst out the door and onto the loading platform, brandishing a sawed-off shotgun.

He spotted Kendra first and swung his weapon around. Paul leaped out from cover and yanked the barrel of the gun upwards, slamming the butt down into the perp's groin. The man doubled up, and Paul tore the shotgun from his grip.

Kendra moved in, sweeping his legs. The man crashed to the ground just as a second perp carrying a pistol rushed outside. His path blocked by his fallen companion, the suspect took aim at Paul.

Kendra shot first. The man grunted in pain, his own bullet going wild. Clutching his chest, he turned to run back inside, but found himself face-to-face with Preston.

"Don't give me a reason," Preston growled.

"No more," he managed through clenched teeth and sagged to his knees beside his prone partner. He placed the pistol on the concrete platform, then assumed the position, locking his hands behind his neck.

"No blood. Suspects must have vests," Paul said. Kendra's gaze remained on the ex-owner of the shotgun.

"Where's Evan Thomas?"

"That bastard sold us out. He and Genaro crawled through the dryer tunnel," he said. "There's a fake panel in the back. If you hurry, you can probably grab them."

As another officer appeared outside to cover them, Preston handcuffed the men. "Go," he said. "We're good here."

Paul followed Kendra inside. One Hartley detective was guarding two employees lying facedown on the floor. He looked up just for a second. "Clear outside?" he asked.

"Yeah," Paul replied, "but we're one perp short, maybe two."

"Let's check the big dryer at the end," Kendra said, "the one with the 'out of order' sign."

Paul opened the door and, glancing inside the stainless steel bin, spotted a nickel-sized piece of green plastic sitting on the drum.

He recognized the device instantly. "It's the GPS tracker you placed on Evan's collar. So where the hell *is* this tunnel?" Paul reached in, put his hand on the circular end of the dryer drum, and pushed. It swung open, revealing an opening beyond.

"I'm going in first." Kendra stepped around him, jumped in, feet first, then eased down into a plywood-lined vertical tunnel. She could see a dim light at the bottom of a ten-foot drop.

She called to Paul. "I think this leads to an adjacent building. Go outside and look around. I'll check things out here."

"Not alone," Paul clipped and, seeing his brother approaching, added, "Preston, I'm backing up Kendra."

"Go. My people will check the surrounding buildings. Maybe we can locate Thomas out there above ground, or find his vehicle," Preston said.

"Copy," Paul said and followed Kendra down.

They were only about ten feet into the three-foot-high, horizontal metal culvert when Kendra entered a side tunnel. Glancing inside, she saw several big metal, ex-military ammo boxes but no suspects. She then heard shuffling ahead and a moan. Though it was hard to see, she could make out a figure leaning against a metal pipe perhaps twenty feet ahead.

She inched forward on her hands and knees, gun ready, and found an injured man pointing a pistol toward the opposite end of the tunnel.

"U.S. Marshal, put down your weapon," Kendra said.

The man eased his grip. The pistol slid out of his hand and clanked onto the metal floor. "Needed to stay alive till you got here…knew you weren't far," he managed in a raspy voice.

"Who are you?" The second Kendra saw the knife still imbedded in his chest, she knew help wouldn't arrive soon enough to save him.

"Use…your cell phone…record…my last words."

Kendra had her phone out and recording within five seconds. "Go ahead," she said, holding the phone close to him.

"My name…Louie Genaro. Thomas, Marshal Thomas, stabbed me. Had the knife hidden in his sling. Traitor…to both sides. Wanted me dead, so he could get away with it, but…not his lucky day."

Genaro's eyes fluttered, but he forced himself to focus again. "Thomas…tried to kill Judge Yolen. I provided…the gun barrel…to replace one on his service weapon just for the kill. Supposed to destroy it later…but kept it…for leverage. Has his prints. My address…in wallet. Look in closet."

She started to ask him more, but Genaro gasped, then his eyes glazed over, and his head sagged onto his chest.

Kendra felt the pulse point at his neck. There was nothing. Aware that Paul had come up from behind, she looked back at him and shook her head. "Did you hear what he said?"

"Yeah. We need to move fast. Thomas isn't getting away this time." His voice, echoing in the tunnel, had grown stone cold.

Kendra placed the cell phone with the recording back in her pocket. "Thomas made a critical mistake when he failed to finish off Genaro. That's going to cost him his freedom and maybe his life."

Paul, taking point, continued down the tunnel and soon pushed up a manhole beside a trash bin. "We're between two buildings," he called back to her, then gave Kendra a hand up.

They ran to the sidewalk and looked around. They were now across the street from the dry cleaners.

"Hey, bro," Preston said, coming up to them.

"Any sign of Thomas?" Paul asked.

Preston shook his head. "Maybe he ducked inside one of the other buildings."

Kendra pointed back to where they'd reached the surface. "We found a small stash of what looks like ammo down there in the tunnel. I didn't see any weapons, though."

"I'll send in an ordnance officer to check it out ASAP," Preston said.

Kendra looked around and located a surveillance camera at the smoke shop just beyond the tiny alley. "Thomas isn't around, so I'm going to assume he drove off. Let's go check their surveillance footage."

The smoke shop owner, who'd gone to high school with one of Paul's brothers, was happy to cooperate.

"There's Thomas," Kendra said, pointing to the image. "Can't miss the sling on his arm. He went straight to that SUV, then headed east."

"I'll put a BOLO out," Preston said. "We'll catch him."

Paul walked outside with Kendra. Just then, Daniel drove up and came to a stop at the curb beside them.

"I've been monitoring police calls and following the events. Don't worry about finding Thomas. He'll find you."

"What do you know that we don't?" Kendra asked.

"If Thomas turns himself in, he's facing the death penalty, so that's not his best option right now. The cartel isn't going to forgive him for bringing the cops here either, and Thomas knows that better than anyone else. The only chance he's got is to convince the cartel that he's still got something to offer. Then he can negotiate a quid pro quo and get their help leaving the country."

"Contacting the cartel at all will be extremely risky for him now, particularly if they find out what he did to Genaro," Kendra said.

"That's my point. He's going to need something really big to convince them of his loyalty and usefulness—like delivering both of you on a platter. The cartel could use two captive marshals as bargaining chips and buy time for the leaders to go to ground."

Kendra drew in a breath. "You're right, Daniel. It's the only deal he's got left."

"That means he'll try to contact us and arrange a meet," Paul said. "I'm guessing he'll approach us with an offer to testify if we can offer him life instead of the death penalty."

"Evan tried to kill a federal judge, and in the process murdered a U.S. Marshal—one of his own. He doesn't have much room to bargain," she said.

"We know that and so does he, but I still think he's going to try. He'll either set us up to be captured or killed by the cartel or maybe convince them he'll do it himself."

"Which means we need a plan," Daniel said. "Come back to my place. Preston will join us there as soon as possible. When Thomas calls, I'll try to zero in on the signal. My equipment is better than what they have at the police department. If you can keep him talking long enough, I can get a location."

"We're assuming he's going to call," Kendra said. "He may decide to go underground on his own."

"If he ends up running from the cops *and* the cartel, his life expectancy goes down to zero," Daniel said.

Paul agreed. "Makes sense to me."

"If he does come after us, we can count on one thing—he won't be alone," Kendra said.

"Neither will we," Paul said. "We'll have all the backup we need."

"Count on that. No way the rest of us guys are going to miss all the fun," Daniel said with a lethal grin.

WHILE PAUL, Gene, Daniel and Preston studied the large, aerial view of Copper Canyon on the computer display, Kendra went into the kitchen for some coffee. She needed to stay completely alert to face what lay ahead.

Paul joined her a moment later. "Preston heard from the DC police. They went to the address Genaro provided. It didn't look like anyone's lived there for a while, but he was telling the truth. They recovered a rifle barrel wrapped in paper and Thomas's prints are on it. If ballistics matches it up with the bullet that killed Judy, Evan's going down."

"I've got some other news," she said. "Tim checked out Evan's whereabouts when your partner was shot and killed. Evan was in DC, ostensibly on personal leave. He wasn't called to respond to the incident, either. He just showed up. Big coincidence, huh?" She placed a hand on his arm. "Looks like you're finally going to have the closure you wanted."

"I know, and there are things I need to say to you once this is over, but until then, there's something I want to give you." Paul reached into his pocket and pulled out a small leather medicine pouch. "I had Daniel pick this up for me. It's from the same Zuñi carver *Hosteen* Silver used to craft our fetishes."

She pulled the tiny figure out carefully. "It's a…deer?" she asked, running her fingers over the delicate carving. It was made from turquoise and beautifully detailed.

"It's Antelope. Antelope people see with their hearts and have the ability and inner strength to accomplish whatever they set out to do," he said. "Antelope will guide you through the fight ahead and beyond."

"I will always keep this with me," she whispered.

"No matter where life takes you, whenever you look at it, think of me," he said, then brushed her face with the palm of his hand.

She leaned into him, allowing herself to bask in that moment of gentleness. "I—" She never got to finish her thought.

Her phone rang, and as Kendra reached for it, Paul's eyes held hers. "If it's Thomas, remember we'll only meet him at Copper Canyon."

Kendra answered, and noting that Paul's brothers had come in and were now watching her, she put the caller on speaker.

"It's Evan," a familiar voice said. "You've always played it smart, Kendra, so think about what I'm going to offer. I can hand over the leaders of the cartel, plus enough evidence to bring them down. In exchange, I want a deal that includes a new identity."

"Go to the Hartley Police Station on Airport Drive right now. We'll meet you there," Kendra said, following the strategy they'd mapped out.

"No way. The cartel's got informants everywhere, including the local P.D. I can't risk showing my face. I'd be as good as dead."

"That's your problem. You betrayed the marshals service. If you want to talk, those are my terms."

"What I'm trading is worth the price I'm asking. You can make your career on a collar like this. Don't throw it away," Evan said. "If you're worried, bring Grayhorse as backup. I've already got a site picked out. Meet me west of Hartley, about a mile down the power plant road."

"No. *I'll* choose the place," she said, then waited several seconds, as if trying to decide. "Meet us at the end of the road that goes up Copper Canyon—that's Grayhorse's old place. There's a big metal gate there. I'll make sure it's unlocked."

He hesitated. "That's a long drive and I'll be a sitting duck every foot of the way."

"Not unless you tell someone where you're going. That

area gets only locals and a little oil worker traffic. That's my offer. Take it or leave it."

"All right." There was a brief pause, then Thomas spoke again. "Meet you there tonight at nine."

As the phone call ended, Kendra looked over at Daniel, who was standing beside his computer. He shook his head. "All we could get was the nearest cell phone tower. At least we know he's still in the area."

"But we knew that already," she said. "At least we got the meeting place we needed."

"I'm bringing two top-notch officers from our tactical unit," Preston said, "and Daniel will provide a few security people and some of their special gear. We'll be ready for whatever surprises Thomas throws in our direction."

"Trust me, and trust us," Paul said. "Tonight you'll have all the trained backup you need, Kendra."

"I know."

As she looked into Paul's eyes, she saw an emotion she didn't dare name reflected in the intensity of his gaze. Everything feminine in her yearned to call it love, to know that her name was forever written in his heart. Yet as a woman and a marshal, she knew that wishes didn't always come true.

She swallowed hard and focused back on business. "Let's go over those plans again."

Chapter Twenty-Two

Traveling at breakneck speed on the gravel roads, Thomas arrived fifteen minutes early. Paul and Kendra heard him long before he showed up on their night vision goggles. The old pickup he'd probably stolen bounced hard on the gravel track and barely made it across the cattle guard of their open gate, clipping a post on the passenger's side.

Despite only having one good arm, Thomas was driving as if the devil himself were chasing him. He nearly wrecked into the trees before he slid to a stop outside the main house.

Paul and Kendra were hidden outside, on the north flank behind some bales of old hay. They stuck to the plan and stayed behind cover, watching as Thomas jumped out of the pickup while it was still running, grabbed something from behind the seat, then sprinted toward the main door. Through his lens, Paul could see Thomas had a handgun at his waist and was carrying his department issue sniper rifle.

Atop the two hundred foot high mesa to their left, above the entrance to the narrow, horseshoe-shaped blind canyon, stood his brother Gene, watching with a powerful spotting scope. "Two SUVs are closing in on Copper Canyon now," Gene said into the mike of his headset. "They just left the highway."

The ranch house door opened just before Thomas reached it. One of Preston's officers greeted Thomas and motioned him into the darkened interior.

"They know what to do with him, right?" Paul spoke quietly into his mike.

"Copy that," Preston said. "Disarm Thomas before he catches on, check him for bugs, then handcuff him and put him in a corner so he can't move or call out until the op's over."

"That's the bad cop part," Kendra whispered, not taking her eyes off the narrow entrance into the blind canyon. "The good part is telling him that if he lives to testify, he might avoid lethal injection."

Paul didn't answer. He was looking to the left, across the floor of the narrow canyon to where Daniel and his two companions were making final preparations.

"The two vehicles have stopped about fifty yards outside the gate," Gene reported. "They're apparently going to advance on foot." There was a pause, then he spoke again. "Four men, wearing ball caps, body armor and night vision gear. I don't see radios, but they could be connected via headsets. All four have assault rifles and spare clips on their belts."

"Copy," Kendra said.

Kendra listened as Daniel and Preston confirmed they were up to speed and ready. Gene, from his overhead observation post, was going to be their eyes and ears. Inside the canyon it was often darker than dark, especially on a night when a moonless sky and the high canyon walls created the deepest of shadows.

"At the gate. They're splitting up, with two men advancing down each shoulder of the road. They're spaced about twenty feet apart," Gene said.

Paul looked over at Kendra, smiled, then pushed his goggles away from his face and clicked on the night scope of his M-4 clone—an assault rifle descended from the old AR-15. Daniel had provided them with the equipment, standard issue for his security training operation. Those, and a few more surprises, would be available if needed.

Paul watched as the first two men walked briskly up on opposite sides of the road, apparently eager to get this over with. He kept his sites on the man farthest from them, knowing that, according to plan, Kendra would be targeting the closer of the two.

Paul spoke into the headset and signaled the house. Behind him a light came on in the cabin. An image silhouetted by a lamp crossed in front of the kitchen window.

The two men closest to them stopped, as did those across the road. Soft words were exchanged, too low to understand, then all four men picked up speed. Soon they were across the road, crouching low and angling toward the house.

A noisy generator started up just then, and three large strobe lights came on, flashing in the faces of the advancing men, blinding their night vision devices. Two of them cursed, raised their weapons and opened fire on the lights. The other two ducked down behind some brush.

Daniel turned on the floodlights next to his position, illuminating the two trying to hide and drawing more misdirected gunfire from the confused attackers.

"We need prisoners," Kendra said. "Don't shoot to kill unless there's no other option."

The spotlighted men fell prone and returned fire, but they were caught in the crossfire, trapped out in the open.

Daniel added hand-directed lasers to his regimen of confusion, forcing the assault team to tear off their night vision devices.

Preston, speaking from beside the house, called out from a bullhorn. "You're surrounded and outgunned. Lay down your weapons."

One of the gunmen whipped his weapon around and fired toward Preston, but someone near Daniel's position took him out with one shot.

Two of the remaining assailants put their weapons down

and sat on the ground, hands locked behind their heads. The fourth set down his rifle but, instead of sitting like the others, suddenly spun around and raced toward the gate.

Kendra jumped up to cut him off, Paul right behind her. The man was fast, but Kendra was between him and the gate. She stopped and fired into the ground right in front of him.

The man tried to dodge, tripped on a prickly pear cactus and fell facedown on the ground.

"Careful now," Paul said, rushing forward, his weapon aimed.

Kendra, barely ten feet from the fallen man, turned her head for a second as Paul came up.

At that instant the man yanked a pistol from his jacket. Kendra caught the motion out of the corner of her eye and swung her weapon around.

Paul fired first. The wounded man clutched his side, dropping his pistol.

"You knew before he even reached for the gun," Kendra said, this time not looking away from the target. "I'm glad you had my back."

"Always." Paul stepped in front of her, standing between her and the gunman, his eyes and weapon still on their assailant.

Kendra and Paul helped the rest of their team collect the captives as a medic tended the man who'd pulled the pistol on Kendra.

After all the prisoners were secured, Kendra went inside the cabin. Thomas was sitting, handcuffed, on the floor, his back against the kitchen counter. "It's over," she said.

"I still want to cut a deal," he said.

"Forget it. You set us up again, but now we have the evidence we need. You're going down this time, Evan, and there won't be a way out."

THREE PHONE CALLS later, however, Evan Thomas *had* struck a deal with the federal prosecutor and had been flown out by state police helicopter to Albuquerque.

"The ones responsible for your partner's death are going away for a long time," Kendra said.

"The fact that Thomas cut a deal doesn't make this feel like a win."

"I know, but he'll still spend life in prison for killing your partner, and look what we got in return. Thomas gave up the names of all his contacts in the weapons cartel and revealed the location of the Colorado mountain hideout used by Garrett Hawthorn, the leader of their operation. He also pinpointed two weapons stashes on a Google map and the entrance of a smuggling tunnel that leads into a Mexican warehouse just across the border. Combined agency strike teams are already en route."

Paul nodded thoughtfully. Deals were everyday compromises in the criminal justice system. "This is the end of a long road."

"Yes it is."

"Time to look to the future," he said, but before he could say more, Kendra was called away to work the scene.

HOURS AFTER the remaining prisoners and the crime scene had been processed, Kendra stood outside the cabin beside her dusty rental car. The sun would be coming up soon and the return trip to Denver would be a long one, so it was time for her to go. Yet she just couldn't make herself leave.

This was the moment she'd dreaded. Prolonging their inevitable goodbye wouldn't help either of them. She'd made her decision. Good friends with benefits would never be enough for her. Working with Paul every day, being part of his world yet knowing that she'd never be at the center of it, would break her heart.

She looked down at her hand, staring at the antelope fetish he'd given her just yesterday. The message was clear. To survive, she had to go.

"What are you doing out here? You getting ready to leave?" he said, coming over to join her.

"Yeah, it's time," she said, and swallowed hard. She'd always stunk at goodbyes.

"It's almost dawn. Can you hold off a bit and come with me? There's a place I want to show you, and we can talk there. Afterwards, if you really want to leave, I won't stand in your way."

"All right," she said. He wasn't going to make leaving easy, but she couldn't find it in her heart to say no. "Where are we going?"

"There's a place that has special meaning to me. I'd like to take you there. It's not far."

He took her hand, and together they walked into Copper Canyon. As the first rays of sunlight fell over the land, small animals stirred in the brush, scampering about in search of food. A hawk flew overhead, idly circling from rim to rim.

As they climbed up a narrow trail that cut into the cliffs, Kendra told herself not to expect anything except one final, beautiful goodbye. Paul had already told her what he was willing to give her—everything, really, except his whole heart. She couldn't expect him to change who he was. She had to accept it and move on.

Soon they reached a ledge that overlooked the canyon floor. He gestured to the vista below them with a sweep of his arm.

"Look to your right," he said. "See that spot that gleams in the sun? That's the metal roof of *Hosteen* Silver's house. About six months after he brought me here, he and I got into an argument. He'd had us carrying water to the livestock and filling two stock tanks hundreds of yards away—by hand. I'd never worked so hard in my life. I accused him of taking us in just for the cheap labor, that he didn't really care about me and Preston."

"Harsh words," she said, eyebrows raised. "What did he do?"

"Nothing. He told me to go check the water in the trough behind the house." He smiled. "He wasn't the kind to explain himself. *Hosteen* Silver felt that by sharing his home and taking care of us, he'd said all that was needed," Paul said. "He was right, but I didn't understand that at the time."

"So what happened?"

"I walked off and came here. I sat down with my feet dangling over the edge and tried to figure out what I should do," Paul said, staring at the shiny metal roof, gleaming like a beacon calling them home. "*Hosteen* Silver tracked me here in less than half an hour."

"Was he angry?"

"No, he just sat down next to me and told me that he'd take me back to the foster home if I wanted to go. If not, I had a family waiting below. The next step was up to me, but if I stayed, I'd have to follow his rules."

Paul paused for several long moments. "That was the first time anyone had ever given me a choice, particularly on something that would determine my future." He turned to face her. "To me, this is a place of beginnings. That's why I wanted to bring you here."

"I'm not sure I understand...."

"It wasn't Lynx who warned me when the gunman you thought was down drew his weapon. I felt the threat to you inside my gut. I acted out of instinct, protecting the woman I love," he said, pulling her into his arms. "Everything that makes me a man tells me you don't want to go, but you think you can't find what you need here." He held her gaze. "Antelope People see with their hearts. Look into mine now. I'm no longer a man chained to the past. When I see you, I see our future. A home, a family, it can all be ours. Say you'll stay with me."

Her whispered yes became nothing more than a sigh as his mouth closed over hers.

Epilogue

Eleven months later

Kendra laughed as Paul dove into the hedge trying to catch the Nerf football flying end over end. Jason, the four-year-old Navajo boy they'd fostered since the death of his single mother, hadn't quite mastered the art of a spiral pass.

"Sorry, pop," Jason yelled, running around the end of the hedge for the ball, which was still out of Paul's reach.

"Paul, you're going to get grass stains all over your knees, and, look at you, Jason. Can't you keep your shoes tied for more than thirty seconds?" Kendra called out, smiling.

Paul laughed, catching Jason's surprise hike as it came over the hedge. "Get back here, boy. Your mom wants us to look our best when we sign those adoption papers today."

Kendra laughed as Paul picked up their feisty soon-to-be son and carried him on his shoulders across the lawn. "Now go put that ball back into the toy box, J.," Paul said, setting him down.

As Jason, the little boy who'd become the love of their lives, raced away, Paul stepped up and gave her a sweet kiss, one hand caressing her swollen belly gently.

"I'm glad we get to make the adoption official before our next little guy arrives," Paul whispered.

"Look on the bright side," Kendra said, resting her head against his chest. "It gave me time to get used to my new job as a working mom." She smiled. "And to think I actually got full maternity leave from your brother Dan so soon after he hired me. That was great."

"It comes from knowing the company's MVP," Paul said, smiling. "Life is as perfect as it can be for us right now, isn't it? I never saw myself as a family man, but now I can't imagine being happy any other way."

She reached up and touched his cheek in a soft caress. "Things didn't always go so smoothly for us. Remember the first time we met? I was stranded and you rescued me at gunpoint. Your confidence was so annoying."

Paul chuckled. "Hey, but in the end, Antelope tamed the Lynx."

"No, not tamed, gentled."

"Maybe so," he murmured, taking her mouth in a kiss as tender as the love that burned in his heart.

* * * * *